UNITED KINGDOM

LONDON ⭐

NETHERLANDS

BELGIUM

ENGLISH CHANNEL

FRANCE

TRAVELS WITH **GANNON & WYATT**

IRELAND

PATTI WHEELER & KEITH HEMSTREET

GREENLEAF
BOOK GROUP PRESS

This book is a work of fiction. Names, characters, businesses, organizations, places, events, and incidents are either a product of the author's imagination or are used fictitiously.

Published by Greenleaf Book Group Press
Austin, Texas
www.gbgpress.com

Distributed by Greenleaf Book Group

For ordering information or special discounts for bulk purchases, please contact Greenleaf Book Group at PO Box 91869, Austin, TX 78709, 512.891.6100.

Design and composition by Greenleaf Book Group
Cover design by Greenleaf Book Group
Cover illustration by Leon Godwin

Publisher's Cataloging-In-Publication Data is available.
ISBN: 978-1-62634-195-1
eBook ISBN: 978-1-62634-196-8

Part of the Tree Neutral® program, which offsets the number of trees consumed in the production and printing of this book by taking proactive steps, such as planting trees in direct proportion to the number of trees used: www.treeneutral.com.

Printed in the United States of America on acid-free paper

15 16 17 18 19 20   10 9 8 7 6 5 4 3 2

First Edition

TreeNeutral

"To live is the rarest thing in the world.
Most people exist, that is all."

Oscar Wilde

"The world is full of magic things, patiently
waiting for our senses to grow sharper."

—William Butler Yeats

ENGLISH/IRISH GAELIC:
TRANSLATION OF COMMON PHRASES

Hello—Dia dhuit

Good morning—Maidin mhaith.

How are you?—Conas tá tú?

I am well—Tá mé go maith

What is your name? Cad is ainm duit?

Yes—Ba mhaith liom

No—Níl

I am sorry—Tá brón orm

Thank you—Go raibh maith agat

It Is foggy—Tá sé ceomhar

It might rain—B'fhéidir go gcuirfidh sé báisteach/
fearthainn

The weather is lovely today—Tá an aimsir
go hálainn inniu

This is great fun—Spórt iontach é seo

Goodnight—Oíche mhaith

Cheers—Sláinte

Ireland Forever!—Éirinn go Brách!

CONTENTS

PART I

A BUNCH OF BLARNEY

GANNON

A couple months back, when my parents told us that we were going to spend our vacation traveling around the Emerald Isle, I had this real funny feeling that the experience might somehow prove life changing. Okay, sure, I always get super excited about visiting a place I've never been, doesn't matter of it's Timbuktu or Katmandu. But there's something about Ireland. Maybe it's that my great-grandparents on my father's side were Irish, which kind of makes me Irish too. Well, part Irish, at least. I wasn't sure exactly how Irish until last week on our flight from New York to Dublin when my detail-obsessed brother actually did the math. He had all these maps and long lists of names and diagrams of family trees spread out all over our tray tables.

"So, after a thorough examination of our family's genealogy," Wyatt said, "I've concluded that you and I are exactly 25 percent Irish."

"That's interesting," I said with a yawn. "Now move all of these papers so I can play some solitaire."

Whatever the exact percentage, we've got a good dose of Irish blood pumping through our veins, and having been here only a short time, I've learned that there's something special about visiting the homeland of your ancestors, knowing that this place—the countryside and farms and castles and music and fables and food—it's all part of who we are.

The country of Ireland sits like a bright green jewel in the North Atlantic Ocean. It's not very big. You can drive from the southern part of the country to the north in about five hour's time. And if you were to count heads along the way, you'd end up at a number somewhere around four and a half million.

The scenic coast of southern Ireland

Small though it may be, Ireland boasts one of the world's most influential cultures. I mean, some of the greatest writers to ever live were from Ireland. Let's see, off the top of my head, there's Bram Stoker, who wrote *Dracula*, James Joyce, W.B. Yeats, Oscar Wilde, George Bernard Shaw, Elizabeth Bowen, Samuel Beckett, and Jonathan Swift, the author of one of my favorites, *Gulliver's Travels*.

The reason Ireland is such a powerhouse of culture, I think, has to do with the magic of the place. And I'm not speaking metaphorically, if that's even the right word. What I mean is that Ireland is a place where magic truly exists. It's well documented in Irish lore and all, but when you are here, standing on Irish soil, you can actually feel it. At random, it will brush up against you, causing your skin to tingle and your hair to stand on end. In these moments, there's a real sense that something otherworldly is at play, something that lies just beyond our own perception.

My brother would say that's all crazy talk, but hey, he's a total science nerd. Kids like him get all hung up on "the facts" and "providing concrete proof" and blah-ba-de-blah-blah, so I wouldn't expect anything less. Me, on the other hand, I'm more open minded. More of a mystic, I guess. Maybe it's that I grew up reading Irish fairy tales and stories of enchanted forests and leprechauns and pots of gold at the end of the rainbow. Whatever it is, I've felt totally dialed into Ireland's magic since we arrived.

That's why tomorrow's visit to Blarney Castle has me so

pumped! For a big talker like me who truly believes in the power of these old legends, there's something special, magical, possibly even life changing to be gained by kissing the Blarney Stone.

We've stopped over for the night in Adare, an old Irish village where cottages and inns have traditional thatched roofs, and horse-drawn carriages take visitors on tours of Adare Manor, one of Ireland's grandest estates.

Adare Manor, County Limerick

My mom and dad are both sleeping like babies in the adjoining room, but poor Wyatt's got his pillow over his face and is complaining that my desk lamp is keeping him up.

Being the nice brother that I am, I guess I'll do him a favor and turn it off. It's probably a good idea to get some shut-eye anyway, since we have to be up at the crack of dawn to catch the bus to County Cork.

Goodnight, Ireland.

Or, as they say in Gaelic, "Oíche mhaith."

WYATT

OCTOBER 3, 6:27 AM
ADARE, IRELAND   52° 33' N   8° 47' W
51° FAHRENHEIT, 11° CELSIUS
GRAY SKIES, A LIGHT DRIZZLE

Each member of my family travels for a different reason.

My dad, he travels in search of inspiration for his paintings and sculptures. After our tour ends, he's headed to a stone cottage he rented on the rocky, windswept coast of the Dingle Peninsula, one of the country's most scenic locations. Ireland boasts "forty different shades of green," and my dad plans to capture every one of them on his canvases. As an artist, this is how he makes a living, but it's also the thing he's most passionate about. He has always told us, find what you love to do and do that thing, because if you do what you love you'll never "work" a day in your life. Pretty good advice, I think.

My mom's been a flight attendant for World Airlines since before Gannon and I were born, so travel is a big part of her job, too. But for her, it's definitely more than just a job. Travel is her passion. She loves to see new places and meet new people. And wherever we go she's willing to lend a helping hand, always volunteering for some cause close to her heart. In a couple days, she's headed back to the capital city, where she'll be working the Dublin-London flights and volunteering at an orphanage on her days off.

I don't want to overlook the fact that my parents also travel for Gannon and me, to introduce us to faraway places, exotic cultures, and the beauty of the natural world. For this invaluable gift, I don't know that I'll ever be able to repay them.

My brother and I travel for different reasons, too. I'm interested in the science of a place: the geology, topography, ecosystem, and climate. I want to understand how it all works, scientifically speaking. Gannon gravitates to the people, their history, culture, and language. He wants to experience what life is actually like for those who live in the places we visit. To walk in their shoes, so to speak.

One thing Gannon and I have in common is what my parents call a *wanderlust*, which basically means we love wandering from one place to the next. We want to see and experience as much of the world as we can. I think Gannon put it best in one of his journal entries when he wrote: "We're on a quest for the kind of knowledge you can't get from a textbook." Actually, that's kind of become our motto.

Cliff of Moher, County Clare

I should close this entry by saying the first week of our visit has been amazing. Ireland is a country of storybook villages, spectacular scenery, good food, and friendly people. What's not to love about it? We've gone rock climbing on the Cliffs of Moher, saw an exciting rugby match in Dublin, and were shown how to carve crystal at a factory in Waterford. We marveled over the magnificent Long Room in the Trinity College Library, which contains original copies of some of the most important books ever written, including the Book of Kells, an elaborately illustrated manuscript created around 800 A.D. We watched the first rays of morning light pierce the inside of

Newgrange, an ancient monument that's actually older than Stonehenge and the Egyptian pyramids. We explored Northern Ireland, which is part of the United Kingdom, stayed in the capital city of Belfast, saw the massive "peace wall" that was built to divide Protestants and Catholics after riots broke out in 1969, and toured the shipyard where the *Titanic* was built. Best of all, we got to visit our great-grandparents' hometown of Castlewellan and learn all about their life as farmers. At night, we've been feasting on shepherd's pie and fish and chips and rich, Irish desserts.

Trinity College Library, Long Room

Life in Ireland has been good.

Real good.

But, as usual, Gannon had to go and mess it all up.

More on that later.

Our shuttle to Blarney Castle departs in ten minutes, and being on time is important to me. Gannon, however, he's the King of Tardiness. I bet he's still in our room snoring like a moose. Actually, I better run back there and make sure he doesn't miss the bus.

GANNON
COUNTY CORK

Around midnight, I woke to a rowdy ruckus.

The kind of rowdy ruckus that involves laughing, singing, and the repeated clinking of glasses. Naturally curious, I crawled from my bed and peeked out the back window only to discover that our cottage was located just across the street from a place called Rooney's Tavern, where merry folks are apparently allowed to carry on into the wee hours of the morning. To each his own, I say, but their good fun kept me up half the night, and I was real foggy in the head this morning and sat alone in the far back of the bus and tried to rest as we rolled through the green hills of southern Ireland toward County Cork.

Funny thing is, the second the bus parked at Blarney Castle, my adrenaline spiked and I literally jumped from my seat and ran for the entrance. As soon as my dad caught up and paid for our tickets, I ripped one out of his hand and took off for the ancient spiral staircase that leads to the top of the castle's tallest tower. The steps were high, the staircase steep and narrow, but I charged ahead, eager to see the magical stone.

"Come on, Wyatt," I said as we wound our way higher. "I'll race you to the top!"

"I'm not racing," Wyatt said. "This staircase is so windy it's making me dizzy."

"Oh, stop your whining. You just know I'd beat you."

Dark gray clouds raced across the sky, carried by a blustery, cold wind that was whipping through the open windows of the castle. Thunder rumbled in the distant hills. We were having some weather, as the Irish like to say. A frigid rain had come down steadily all morning, making the unbelievably narrow staircase about as slippery as an ice rink.

"Hurry up, Mom and Dad!" I shouted.

"We're coming!" I heard them say from somewhere down below.

"Okay! We'll meet you at the top!"

Blarney Castle, County Cork

Atop the castle tower is a walkway that runs all the way around the barrier wall. The center is open to a courtyard below, its stonewalls crawling with ivy and moss. Looking out over the tower spires I noticed just how high we were, well above the tallest trees.

"Blarney Castle was built in the 1400s by Cormac McCarthy, King of Munster," Wyatt read from the pamphlet he'd been given when we bought our tickets. "The castle's high walls of stone served as his stronghold for years, housing knights and guards and protecting him from enemy attack."

Gazing over the countryside, I could almost imagine an invading army surrounding the castle, hundreds of men on horseback shooting arrows up and over the walls.

"Read on," I said. "What's it say about the Blarney Stone?"

"The Blarney Stone is shrouded in mystery. Some claim it was the stone Moses struck to provide water for the Israelites. Others say it was the deathbed pillow of Saint Columba, the patron saint of those who love books. Yet others say Scottish kings regarded it as the stone of destiny. Whatever the stone's history, it has long been believed that kissing it gives one the gift of eloquence, or, as it is more commonly known, the *gift of gab*."

"I told you, Wyatt. It's all true."

The way I saw it, kissing the stone would give me the verbal skills to win any debate, woo crowds, basically convince anyone of anything.

"It's all a bunch of rubbish is what it is," Wyatt said as he slid the pamphlet back into his coat pocket. "A long time ago, someone made up the whole story just to sell tickets to suckers like you."

"Hey, you bought a ticket too," I said.

"I just came up for the view."

My parents finally made it to the top.

"I don't think that staircase is built to code," my dad said.

"There isn't even a railing. Imagine walking up those steps in a full suit of armor. I don't know how the knights did it."

"It's cold up here," my mom said, burying her hands in her pockets.

"Pucker up, Gannon," Wyatt said. "I'm ready to warm up by a fire with a cup of hot tea."

"I'm with you, Wyatt," my mom added as she nuzzled into my dad. "So, where is this famous stone anyway?"

"Follow me," I said.

We walked to the other side of the tower where a man was seated by a square hole in the walkway. The Blarney Stone is set into the barrier wall 90 feet above the ground. It's a rectangular piece of smooth rock that's a slightly lighter shade than the wall itself and sits about two feet below the walkway.

The magical Blarney Stone

"So, how do I get my lips on this thing?" I asked.

"Oh, it's easy, laddy," the man said. "Lie on your back facing away from the stone and lower your head into the hole. When you see the stone, kiss it."

"Wait a sec. I have to hang upside down? What if I fall through the hole?"

"That's what the safety bars are for. See 'em?"

I saw them all right. They were thin and spaced so far apart it looked like I could slip right between them.

"I'd rather not test them out," I said.

"Then don't fall," the man said with a smirk.

This guy had a good sense of humor.

"My name's Gannon," I said, extending my hand. "It means 'fair-haired one' in Gaelic."

"William McGuiness," he said as we shook.

"So, Mr. McGuiness. Any famous people ever kiss this stone?"

"Oh, many, lad. The famous writer and explorer Sir Richard Francis Burton, rock 'n' roll legend Mick Jagger, even the great statesman Sir Winston Churchill."

"No, way! You hear that, Mom and Dad? Winston Churchill kissed the Blarney Stone."

"So when you kiss the stone it's kind of like you're kissing Winston Churchill," Wyatt said.

"Thanks for the visual, Wyatt," I replied.

"Don't mention it."

"I think Churchill's lips have long since washed away,

lad," Mr. McGuiness said. "You've got a line forming behind you. Do you want to kiss the stone or not?"

"Okay, let's get on with it," I said and handed my video camera to my mom.

I sat down on the wet walkway and turned my back to the stone. My mom pointed the video camera at me.

"Is it rolling?" I asked her. "I have a few words I'd like to say."

"It's rolling!" my mom answered.

I cleared my throat and spoke loudly so that I would be heard over the wind.

"Oh, ye great spirits of the Blarney!"

"Oh ye?" Wyatt repeated, making a face.

"Shut it, Wyatt. Take two. From the top." I cleared my throat again. "Oh, ye great spirits of the Blarney! I come before you today to humbly request that upon pressing my lips to this stone, I am granted the gift of eloquence. The gift of verbal persuasiveness. The gift of . . ."

"Kiss the thing already!" Wyatt yelled.

A few people waiting in line chuckled.

"Okay," I said, giving a nod to Mr. McGuiness. "It's go time!"

I leaned back and he helped me slide over the hole. Carefully, I arched my back and dropped my head lower. My whole world turned upside down. It felt like every ounce of blood in my body was rushing into my brain all at once. My vision went blurry and I got real disoriented.

"Give it a big smacker and I'll help you up," Mr. McGuiness said.

"And try not to catch any germs!" Wyatt yelled. "Over 300,000 people kiss the Blarney Stone every year, in case you were wondering!"

I'm not going to lie, the idea that hundreds of thousands of people put their lips on this thing every year was a bit of a problem for me.

"Do you ever disinfect this stone?" I asked Mr. McGuiness, while still hanging upside down.

"I clean it after every kiss," he said.

"Oh, good," I said, relieved.

"That was a joke, laddy."

By this point my face felt like an overinflated balloon. The pressure in my head was so intense it seemed possible that my eyeballs might just pop right out of the sockets.

"You hang upside down much longer and you might pass out," Mr. McGuiness said. "I suggest you get intimate with this rock or give the next person their turn."

"Go for it, Gannon!" I heard my mom shout. "Give that stone a big smooch!"

"Okay, okay!" I yelled. "Here I go!"

Very slowly, I extended my quivering lips. The instant I felt the faintest touch of that cold, germy stone against them, I pulled my head away. Mr. McGuiness helped me up and I sat there in a daze.

"Was it everything you'd hoped it would be?" he asked with a smile.

"I think so," I said. "Thanks for your help."

"My pleasure, lad. Who's next?"

When I stood up, a head rush sent me staggering into the wall.

I braced myself and waited for the castle to stop spinning.

"Well, congratulations," my dad said. "You did it."

"Let's see if it worked," Wyatt added. "Go ahead, Gannon. Say something brilliant."

I took a deep breath and tried to gather my thoughts. A long, drawn out, "Uhhhhhh" was all I could muster.

Wyatt burst out laughing.

"Oh, that's perfect," he said. "So eloquent. What did I tell you? It's just a myth. You just proved it, Gannon."

I held up my finger, gesturing to Wyatt that I needed another minute.

"I have a theory," Wyatt continued. "Let's say you have someone who already talks way too much. And let's say this loudmouth kisses the Blarney Stone. Could it be that the effect is reversed? Instead of the 'gift of gab' maybe this person is hit with a curse. The curse of silence. Can you imagine what it would be like if Gannon suddenly became speechless? Let's be honest, it'd be a curse for him but a gift to all of us."

My mom frowned at Wyatt, but he just continued to laugh his head off. Man, was he getting a kick out of himself.

"Let's head back down and warm up," my mom said, handing me my video camera. "Our bus leaves in thirty minutes."

I think I can chalk up my lack of verbal eloquence this afternoon to that whole head rush thing. Most important is that I've actually kissed the stone, so I'm pretty sure the gift of gab will be granted to me soon enough.

All in all, I have to say, the first part of our trip to Ireland has been totally awesome! And the best is yet to come. Okay, Wyatt's opinion may differ from mine a little bit, but I think he'll change his tune once he's had a taste of what I know will be a "true Irish experience."

WYATT

OCTOBER 4, 1:57 PM
KILLARNEY, IRELAND 52° 03′ N 9° 30′ W
54° FAHRENHEIT, 12° CELSIUS
GRAY SKIES, DRIZZLE

I feel the need to amend my previous journal entry by saying that our *wanderlust* doesn't always result in an ideal travel experience. Fact is, it sometimes lands us in very uncomfortable situations. Our current situation would be a perfect example.

A few days ago we paid a visit to the Youth Exploration Society Dublin office to learn about some of the adventures offered in the area. To fill our remaining time in Ireland, my parents had given us the task of finding a project that was educational. While we were at the Y.E.S. office, we were told about a program that assigns young students to a farm where they work in the fields and learn all about organic agriculture. Of course, Gannon went nuts over this idea and insisted that we sign up.

"Come on, Wyatt," Gannon said. "You have to admit, this has been a pretty cushy trip so far. We haven't really gotten our hands dirty, so to speak."

"Cushy isn't always a bad thing."

"Well, I dislike feeling at home when I am abroad. You know who said that?"

"Uh-uh."

"Didn't think so. It was George Bernard Shaw. One of Ireland's greatest writers. He won the Nobel Prize, which is pretty much the highest honor for a writer."

I was hoping Gannon would let it go, but that was just wishful thinking.

"Just say yes and let's get on with it, Wyatt. Learning how to run an organic farm would be so awesome!"

"Sorry, I just don't know that I agree with you," I said.

"How could you not agree with me? Farming is something very few young people know how to do these days. Think about it, if we couldn't buy food at the grocery store, most of the world would go to bed with an empty stomach. We should all know how to live off the land, how to plant a field of seeds and help them sprout and mature and bloom into a garden of nutritious fruits and vegetables. This is important stuff, bro. Besides, our ancestors were Irish farmers. Aren't you curious what life was really like for them way back then?"

"Eh," I said.

"Don't 'eh' me. I'm talking about agriculture here. And agriculture is a science . . . isn't it?"

"It is."

"That's what I thought. So, given that it's a science, a farm is the perfect place for you. Seriously, you can nerd-out all you want. Study the germination of a potato or a cabbage or whatever. The boring things you do to fill your time are totally up to you. All I'm saying is that we'll both learn a lot and have a great time doing it. It'll be a real Irish experience!"

It is true, farming is a big part of our family's history. And yes, it is still an important part of Irish culture. The temperate climate is ideal for growing crops and raising livestock. The countryside is spectacularly green. At least it is when the sun manages to break through the clouds, which, unfortunately, is not all that often this time of year. Hillsides are dotted with stone cottages. Waist-high rock walls, built during the great famine, divide the landscape into geometrical patterns. Turn your head in almost any direction and you'll see sheep.

Gannon did have a point. Working on an Irish farm would be educational, and I'm always up for learning something new. In addition, this sort of experience would serve our journals well. Because we travel so much, we're homeschooled by my mom and our journals are a big part of our writing grade. An experience on the farm would definitely give us good material, both scientific and cultural, and I was sure the Youth Exploration Society would consider publishing our field notes as long as they met the society's high standards.

Combine all of that with the fact that Gannon wouldn't stop nagging me until I gave him an answer, and I felt inclined to give in.

"Come on, Wyatt," Gannon said. "You know Mom and Dad will love this program. It fits into our homeschool studies perfectly! So, what'll it be, bro? Yes or no? I need an answer. Clock's ticking. Come on, yes or no? Huh? Yes or no?"

"Fine, Gannon," I said. "If you'll just stop talking, I'll do it."

"Oh, yeah!" he said, pumping his fist. "Consider these lips zipped. Not going to say another word about it. I promise."

Goes without saying, but Gannon's promise was an empty one.

Thinking back, I can't actually remember a time when giving in to a whim of my brother's has worked out well for me, and this time is proving no different. I can't even believe I'm writing this, but right now we're riding in the back of a flatbed truck, crammed into a small, cold space that we happen to be sharing with a few dozen caged chickens. I'm huddled in the corner, wrapped in an itchy and awful smelling blanket while hundreds of chicken feathers swirl around in the air.

Gannon is sitting in the opposite corner, talking to the chickens. You can't make this stuff up. He has his Gaelic-English dictionary open on his lap and is practicing some common phrases on them. The chickens must think he's a lunatic. I know I do.

All of us—Gannon, myself, and the chickens—are en route to a farm. The farm is owned by a Mr. Cormac O'Leary, the same man who so generously arranged our transportation via this traveling hen house. Mr. O'Leary manages the farm with his daughter, Grace, who we were told is close to our age. They grow potatoes, cabbage, and an assortment of other vegetables. They also raise sheep, chickens (obviously), and have a reforestation project in the works on a large section of the family land.

Their farm is where we'll be working. Tending to the land, feeding the animals, shearing sheep, and helping with the reforestation, among other things. It's no "cushy" vacation, and that was the original purpose of us visiting Ireland. But looking back on my family's travel history, it seems we're always stepping out of our comfort zone and seeking experiences that are unique, as I mentioned before. This being the case, I guess I shouldn't have expected anything less in Ireland.

At this point, I am just trying to stay positive and make the most of the experience. Looking around at all these stinky, clucking chickens, I imagine things can only get better. It seems impossible that they could get any worse.

Connemara National Park

GANNON

Okay, fine, I'll admit it. Life on the farm hasn't quite turned out to be all that I thought it would. I mean, it's actually hard work. A heck of a lot harder than I imagined. And this is only day one. So, let's see . . . thirty minus one . . . cross out the three, put the one in front of the zero . . . yep, that's what I thought. Twenty-nine days to go.

Deep breath.

In through the nose, out through the mouth.

Repeat.

Okay, so where was I?

Ah, that's right. Standing in the cold, mud-soaked Irish countryside, drenched from head to toe and shivering while my brother whines like a baby.

"I just want to state for the record that this is all your fault," Wyatt said.

"Let's not go pointing fingers," I shot back.

Ignoring my request, Wyatt pointed his finger right in my face.

"I'll point fingers if I want," he said.

"Hey, you wanted to come to Ireland as much as I did. We've both had this country near the top of our travel list forever."

"It's not Ireland that's bothering me. Ireland is great. I

love Ireland! It's the fact that we're working on this farm, sunup to sundown, in this cold and rain and filth. And it was all *your* idea. Therefore, it is all *your* fault. Sorry, but it's impossible to dispute that logic."

I'd had just about enough of my brother's crummy attitude.

"You know what, Wyatt?" I said.

"What?"

"Póg amach."

Wyatt crinkled his eyebrows.

"Pog a-*what*?" he said.

"Póg amach."

"What does that mean?" he asked.

"It's Gaelic. Look it up."

"Hey now!" came a voice from the patio. "No more of that talk on this farm, lad! You got it?"

"Tá brón orm, Mr. O'Leary," I said, which means "I'm sorry."

"My daughter returns tomorrow evening from an overnight camp in the mountains of Connemara," Mr. O'Leary continued. "Part of her environmental education class. Next week school is out for fall holiday, so she'll be at the farm mostly. Anything but the best behavior around her and we're going to have a problem. You follow?"

"Yes, sir," I said.

"Now get back to work. Last I checked, these weeds don't pluck themselves. Or was I mistaken?"

"No, sir. You're not mistaken."

"Didn't think so."

Mr. Cormac O'Leary is a tall, slightly weathered, partially freckled, and supremely crotchety old Irishman. Looking the part of a lifelong farmer, he wears mud-stained overalls, a gray wool sweater, and a tweed coat that is worn on the lapels and has leather patches on the elbows. Atop a graying head of hair sits a wool driving cap. My guess is that he's around fifty years old, but I don't have the nerve to ask.

"Sir, if I may," Wyatt said, catching Mr. O'Leary before he returned to the barn.

"What is it, lad?"

"It's just that I've given our situation some thought."

"Oh, have you now?"

"Yes, sir. I have. And I've concluded that we can't really make much progress today due to all this rain."

"Now don't go using the rain as an excuse for your laziness," Mr. O'Leary said, turning his head and spitting into the muck. "Weather is weather. We don't control it. Am I right? You don't control Mother Nature, do you? Because if you do, that'd mean you must be some sort of teenage incarnation of the great God Almighty. And if you are the good Lord above, I've got much bigger problems I'd like for you to tackle before we address the weather! So, tell me, lad. Are *you* the great God Almighty?"

"No," Wyatt said.

"Pardon me?" Mr. O'Leary said, cupping his hand behind his ear.

"No, sir. I'm not."

"That's right you're not, which means that you don't control Mother Nature. None of us do. That's why we must learn to work with her."

Oh, man, was I loving this. Wyatt was getting a good ole' fashioned verbal lashing, but still, he couldn't let it go. Apparently, he believed his "logical" reasoning would win over Mr. O'Leary. I'm very happy to report that he was wrong.

"I'm just thinking maybe we should take a break and get back to work when the rain stops," Wyatt said. "Have you seen the forecast? Maybe it's supposed to clear up soon."

"I don't need anyone to tell me the forecast," Mr. O'Leary said. "It's always the same."

"It is?" I said, curious as to how that could be.

"In Ireland it rains twice a week. The first time for three days, and the second time for four days."

It took me a few seconds to do the math.

"Oh, I get it," I said with a chuckle. "You're basically saying it rains all week, right?"

"It's a small wonder you figured that out, lad," Mr. O'Leary said with a smirk. "Take it from me, this rain is nothing. Just wait till it buckets down. Now, crack on. Tomorrow you'll get a fine education in manure."

"Looking forward to it," Wyatt said.

"Yeah, can't wait," I added.

"It'll be a gas," Mr. O'Leary said, and let out a good belly laugh as he turned and slopped off through the squishy soil toward the barn.

"How did our great-grandparents do this?" Wyatt asked.

"I have no idea, but it's safe to say that neither of us inherited their farming skills."

Okay, so maybe committing to a month of hard labor on a farm was a bit of a mistake, but I've given my word, and when Gannon gives his word it's as good as gold. Well, silver, at least. Maybe bronze on my worst days. Anyway, there's a lot for us to learn on this farm, can't deny that. So, no matter how bad it gets, I plan to stick it out to the end.

Only twenty-nine days to go.

Ugh!

WYATT
OCTOBER 4, 9:37 PM
COUNTY KERRY, IRELAND
47° FAHRENHEIT, 8° CELSIUS
WIND 10-15 MPH, RAIN

It's only been a day and my hands are blistered, my muscles ache, and the chill I got standing around in the cold rain sank so deep into my bones I don't know that I'll ever shake it. And tomorrow we get to do it all over again. And the next day too. And the day after that. And so on and so forth for far too long.

It's clear that Mr. O'Leary has every intention of getting

all the labor he can out of us. Seeing as how I only just met the man, I will withhold judgment. But if first impressions are a true indicator of one's personality, Mr. O'Leary is about as charming as a rabid weasel.

I have plenty more to write about all this, but at the moment I'm lacking energy and need to lie down. In closing, I have just one thing left to say: My brother is a dead man!

GANNON

Sheep grazing in the field

You know, before actually doing the job of a "manure spreader" I would have guessed that it might rank up there as one of the top three worst jobs I've ever had, right behind cleaning the toilets on a ship in British Columbia and digging holes in the scorching Egyptian desert, but turns out I was wrong. The job of manure spreader is undoubtedly, undeniably, and without question *the* worst job I have ever had.

Some of the manure was dry and dusty and would blow right in my face when I spread it on the soil, and then there was the manure that Mr. O'Leary called "fresh," which was damp and mushy, and well, let's just say this, once the job is finished, my gloves should be tossed into a bonfire.

Amazing that this stuff is actually used to fertilize crops. Crops we eat! Sorry, but the whole idea just doesn't sit well with me, or my stomach.

I had spread what seemed like my hundred and fiftieth wheelbarrow onto the soil and was headed back to the barn to reload when a soft, rhythmic melody caught my attention. It seemed to be coming from inside the O'Leary's house.

"Did I tell you you're a dead man yet?" Wyatt said. "Even if I did, I'll go ahead and say it again. You are a dead man."

"Be quiet for a sec," I said. "You hear that?"

The sound was mesmerizing, like the footsteps of fairies dancing across the leaves of an enchanted forest.

"I do," Wyatt said. "What is it?"

"Pretty sure it's the national symbol of Ireland," I said.

"And what would that be?"

"The harp."

Now, I'm not bragging or anything, but I have a real

ear for music. Don't get me wrong, I can't play a note of it myself, but I do know good music when I hear it, and the sound coming from the farmhouse could fill the seats of Carnegie Hall.

"You don't think that's Mr. O'Leary playing, do you?" Wyatt asked.

"He doesn't seem like the harp-playing type."

I became lost in the tune, soothed and comforted by it to the point that I almost forgot I was covered head to toe in mud and dung. By the time the music stopped, I was in a trance.

Suddenly, the front door of the farmhouse swung open, snapping me back to reality. Through it walked a young girl about our age. She wore a heavy denim coat, jeans, and knee-high rain boots. A colorful wool scarf hung from her neck. Firelight filled the windows of the farmhouse, casting a warm glow over her strawberry blonde hair.

"Whoa," I whispered. "It's like an angel just appeared before us."

Brushing myself off the best I could, I walked toward the girl. As we came closer to each other, her eyes just about stopped me dead in my tracks. They were blue like glacial ice and radiated against the ashy-gray sky.

"Hi, I'm Gannon," I said, my voice cracking slightly.

"Hello," she said with a smile. "I'm Grace."

"Mr. O'Leary's daughter."

"The one and only."

As if her spectacular eyes weren't enough, Grace had a beautiful Irish accent.

"It's really great to meet you," I said.

Offering my hand, I noticed a leather glove on her left arm that ran all the way to her elbow. "I hope you're not offended if I don't shake your hand," she said. "Da tells me you've had a long day in the fields."

"Oh, yeah," I said, lowering my filthy hand. "Of course."

"And you must be Wyatt," she said.

"Nice to meet you," Wyatt said as he approached.

"Don't pay any attention to him," I said. "Was that you playing the harp?"

"Yes, it was."

"I've never heard anything like it. I'm being serious. You have a real talent."

"You're very kind," she said, blushing. "My ma taught me when I was a little girl."

Her attention was drawn suddenly to something within the forest.

"Excuse me a minute," she said, stepping aside.

She held up her gloved hand and whistled. I was curious what she was doing when out of nowhere a rush of wind passed over me. I ducked my head and jumped out of the way, and as I did caught sight of a huge bird, its wings fanned wide, razor sharp talons extended. It swooped in and landed on Grace's forearm.

"What the—" I said. "Is that an eagle?"

"No, it's not an eagle," she said.

"Wait, let me guess." I thought for a few seconds. "It's a falcon!"

"That's correct. A red-tailed falcon."

"Is it your pet or something? Because if it is, it's the most awesome pet ever."

Grace laughed.

"I would call him a friend more than a pet," she said. "We found him the summer I trained at the School of Falconry at Ashford Castle. He had injured his wing and we nursed him back to health. They allowed me to bring him to the farm to release him. Guess he likes it here, because he's been hanging around ever since."

"Does he have a name?" I asked.

"I named him Oscar, after one of my favorite Irish writers, Oscar Wilde."

Oscar was a sleek, aerodynamic bird with shiny brown feathers. His eyes were small and brown and he had a pointy yellow bill that was hooked at the end. His wings must have spanned four feet, at least.

"You know, I've always wanted to learn falconry," I said to Grace. "Maybe you could teach me."

"I'd be happy to."

One of the feathered residents of Ashford Castle

Mr. O'Leary hollered to us from the front porch.

"Dinner is served!" he said, and stepped back into the house.

"Perhaps you and Wyatt would like to wash up first," Grace said.

"Yeah, I think that might be a good idea," I said, holding up my soiled hands.

Grace stepped aside and said goodnight to Oscar. Lifting

her arm, the falcon took flight and was soon swallowed whole by the darkness of the forest.

"I'll see you inside," she said.

"Okay," I said. "We won't be long."

As Grace strolled back toward the farmhouse, I couldn't take my eyes off her. "Wow," I said quietly to myself. "What an amazing girl."

Washing up, I had a permanent grin on my face. I mean, getting to know Grace will be well worth whatever crummy jobs Mr. O'Leary has planned for us. Seriously, all the long, hard days we have left on the farm, well, they don't look so bad after all.

WYATT

OCTOBER 5, 8:06 PM
45° FAHRENHEIT, 7° CELSIUS
WIND 5-10 MPH, LIGHT RAIN

Seated around a table in a warm, candlelit room, we all enjoyed a delicious home-cooked meal. Traditional Irish fare was served—a tender beef stew loaded with potatoes, carrots, and celery, along with a heaping basket of buttermilk biscuits to dip in the thick broth. Packed with protein, carbohydrates, and fats, it's just the kind of hearty meal a body craves after a long day on the farm.

"You all have quite an evening in store tomorrow," Mr.

O'Leary said as he took a bite of a biscuit. "Make sure your finest clothes are in order."

"Why's that, Mr. O'Leary?" Gannon asked.

"After you finish fertilizing the crops," he said, "I'm taking you all to the Francis Bacon exhibit at Dromoland Castle."

"Oh, Da!" Grace shouted, clapping her hands together. "Thank you! Thank you! Thank you!"

"Ah, don't get so worked up. It's nothing. Martin, the castle butler, he owes me a favor, that's all. Said he'd be happy to have you all to the event as his guests."

"I'm sorry, but who is Francis Bacon?" I asked, reluctantly.

"Oh, just one of the greatest painters the world has ever known," Mr. O'Leary said. "An Irish-born chap."

"Forgive my brother," Gannon said. "When it comes to art, he knows about as much as that biscuit you're eating."

Grace smiled.

"Among art collectors, Francis Bacon's work is some of the most sought after in the world," Grace said. "It's right up there with Van Gogh, Monet, and Picasso."

"And these aren't just any Bacon paintings," Mr. O'Leary continued. "It's one of his most famous works, 'Three Studies of Lucian Freud.' It's being sold at auction. The work is a bit odd looking, if you ask me, but these paintings are certainly a big deal if you're into that kind of thing."

"I read in the newspaper that the paintings are expected to set a record for the highest price ever paid for a work of art," Grace said.

"So, how much are they supposed to sell for?" I asked.

"One hundred and twenty million, the experts say. Possibly more."

I nearly choked on my milk.

"One hundred and twenty million *dollars*?" I asked, wiping the milk from my chin.

"No, a hundred and twenty million *potatoes*, Wyatt," Gannon said.

Apparently Grace appreciates sarcasm, as Gannon's comment got a good laugh out of her.

"It's hard to believe," Mr. O'Leary said, almost to himself as he stirred his stew with a spoon. "Hard to believe."

"I don't think I've ever seen anything worth that much money," Gannon said.

"Not many people have," Grace said.

"All I ask is that you be on your best behavior," Mr. O'Leary said. "I know Gracie will act accordingly. It's you two mugs I'm worried about. Even though you aren't blood relation, you'll be representing the O'Leary family, and I want our name to remain well respected. Is that understood?"

"Understood, sir," I said.

"Absolutely," Gannon chimed in.

"It's a bit of a drive to get there," Mr. O'Leary continued. "All the way up in County Clare. I'll be towing the tractor up to Galway to have the engine repaired anyhow, so I can drop you off. I'll probably stay overnight in the city, drive back the next morning. Martin said he will take you home."

"Thanks a lot, Mr. O'Leary," Gannon said. "I can't wait to see these paintings. And I promise. We'll be on our absolute best behavior."

To attend such an exclusive event is quite an opportunity, but I have one small concern. It's Gannon. I know he promised Mr. O'Leary he would behave, but if I know my brother, that's a promise he's going to have a hard time keeping.

GANNON
LATE NIGHT

After a delicious meal, we made tea and sat in the living room as Mr. O'Leary stoked the fire.

"I'll make you a cup, Mr. O'Leary," I said. "How would you like it?"

"Two sugars and a drop of milk," he said.

"Coming right up."

"Go raibh maith agat, Gannon," Mr. O'Leary said, which means, "thank you."

Grace came back from her room with a thick scrapbook, and we all gathered around. On the front cover was a black and white photo of a woman in a white dress. She had a humble smile and was glancing at the camera from an angle, giving the impression that she was shy. Her hair was blonde and her skin fair, similar to Grace. She looked to be in her thirties.

"I take it this is a photo of your mother," I said.

"Yes," Grace said, solemnly. "I made this book just after she passed."

"What was her name?" I asked.

"Kaitlin."

"She's beautiful."

Grace's eyes glazed over with tears as she turned the page.

"This is my ma when she was a child," Grace said, pointing to a grainy black and white image that was weathered around the edges. "She must have been five or six years old." Next to her a small tree stood in the soil, just a seedling really. "That's the day she planted the Scots pine on the hill behind the house."

"Yeah, I saw that tree," I said, having noticed the Scots pine earlier in the day. It stands all alone, towering into the sky, and has a trunk as wide around as the wheel of a tractor. "Wow, it's amazing to think that the little twig in this picture became that giant tree out there."

"Reminds me of Ma every time I look at it," Grace said. "She was the first in her family to understand the importance of reforestation. There was a time when almost all of Ireland's native forests had been cut down. Even the beautiful national forest that backs up to the western edge of our property was under threat. She helped make sure it was protected, and even replanted over half of our family's two hundred hectares with native trees. Though she is gone, her presence still surrounds us."

The lone Scot's pine on the hillside

Grace's grandparents had only one child, Kaitlin, and were thrilled when she married Cormac, a strong, able-bodied man who grew up herding sheep and could be of help around the farm. Cormac and Kaitlin moved into the small cottage behind the main house and together helped make the farm one of the most productive in all of County Kerry.

"Kaitlin, God rest her sweet soul," Mr. O'Leary said, pausing to glance at the heavens, "her family, the Flanagans, they owned this land for six generations. Gave it the name Shamrock Farm over two hundred years ago and it's been productive ever since. Even survived the great famine in the mid-1800s, when over one million Irish people died of starvation. Now Gracie and I are the last ones, and I'm not leaving until they carry me off in a wooden box."

"Don't talk like that, Da," Grace said, swatting him on the shoulder.

"I'm not expecting it to happen anytime soon, God willing," he said. "I intend to be around until you've filled this farm with your own wee little ones."

"You'll be one of those grumpy grandpas sitting on the porch in your rocker, barking orders at everyone, won't you?" Grace said with a smile.

"As well I know it," Mr. O'Leary said with a laugh.

"This is one of my favorite pictures," Grace said, pointing out a photo of her mother standing along a river with the Eiffel Tower in the distance.

"Oh, cool," I said. "Paris."

"It was my mother's favorite city," she said. "She and my da visited when they were younger."

"That trip to Paris filled her head with ideas," Mr. O'Leary said. "She came home and wrote poetry for weeks. When the inspiration of the city wore off, she'd disappear into the forest. She saw one of the last wolves to ever tread Irish soil in that forest. Morning to night sometimes, I wouldn't see her. Then, emerging from the trees, up the hill she'd come, a smile on her face. Good gracious, when she'd get into her writing it became a challenge to get her to do anything else. But she always did what needed to be done on the farm, and she did it well. She did everything well."

I turned to Wyatt and whispered: "I wonder if she ever saw a leprechaun in the forest."

"Don't you dare ask," Wyatt said, quiet but stern, then quickly changed the subject.

"So, your mom was a poet?" he asked.

"She was," Grace said.

"So is Grace," Mr. O'Leary said. "Gets it from her ma, obviously."

"Poetry and music are my greatest passions," Grace said. "When I'm older, I'd like to study both at university. What about the two of you? Do you think you'll ever settle down enough to attend college?"

"Oh, sure," I said. "I want to study filmmaking. Maybe creative writing, too."

"Science for me," Wyatt said. "Anthropology, zoology, maybe minor in biology or botany. Not really sure yet."

I faked a yawn.

"After university, I'd like to spend some time traveling, just like you've been doing," Grace said. "I'd love to see Paris, of course. And I've always had a fascination with Australia. Maybe it's the kangaroos and koala bears. Or the sunshine and warm weather. I don't know, but I'm determined to visit one day."

Mr. O'Leary abruptly tossed his napkin aside.

"Agh, travel is rubbish."

"That's not true, Da. You're just being cranky. And you know Ma always encouraged me to get out and see the world."

"But don't forget what else your ma said. You can learn just as much about life wandering around in that forest, observing nature—the birds and the trees and the rocks—as you can doing anything else."

"And that's just one of the reasons you know I'll return, Da. My heart will forever be here. On this land with you."

"Ah, don't make me weepy now," Mr. O'Leary said, dabbing the corner of his eye with a handkerchief. He gathered himself and turned to us. "Just to make sure she does return, I have a plan. I'm going to build Grace a small cottage overlooking the pond. A cozy writing studio with a wide desk, a stone fireplace, and bookshelves against the wall. A place where she can spend the days focused on her poetry. Grace has talent. That she does. Mark my words, lads, one day her name will be mentioned in the same breath as Joyce, Yeats, and Shaw."

"Any chance you'd read us one of your poems?" I asked.

"Oh, I don't think so," Grace responded.

"Please."

"Read them the one you wrote about your ma," Mr. O'Leary said. "It's my favorite."

"No, I'd really rather not."

"Oh, Gracie, you must. After all this talk of your ma, my heart yearns for those words. Please find that beautiful poem and read it to us."

Grace paused to consider the request.

"I don't need to find it," she said, finally. "I have it committed to memory."

Grace looked at the ground and took a deep breath through her nose. After a moment, she straightened her posture, looked at us, and spoke. I can't remember every word, but the poem ended something like this:

"To love and be loved,

there is no more noble claim,

A child to a mother,

A flower to the rain."

"You seriously wrote that?" I asked once she had finished. She smiled, nodding humbly.

"Jeez, Mr. O'Leary, you were right," I said. "You might just have a future Nobel Prize winner in the family."

"That I might, lad," he said, dabbing tears from his eyes. "That I might."

I could have sat there for several more hours, but it was getting late. Eventually Mr. O'Leary put out the fire, and we all wished one another a good night's sleep. Honestly, I couldn't imagine a more pleasant ending to an otherwise unpleasant day.

WYATT

The hard rain that battered the windowpane early this morning had slowed to a drizzle by the time we made our way to the field. It was still plenty wet but slightly warmer than yesterday. I spent the morning spreading fertilizer and was just about to break for lunch when I noticed an area of crops that were wilted. Lots of the leaves had turned black around the edges. Making my way toward the river, I found an even larger area of damaged crops. Some, it seemed, were already dead.

I called Mr. O'Leary over to take a look. He knelt down in the field of cabbage and inspected the withered leaves.

"This is no good," he said to himself.

From there, we inspected the potatoes. Just like the cabbage, most of the leaves were darkened and wilted. When Mr. O'Leary pulled a few potatoes from the ground, they had round, black spots on them, similar to bruises.

Historically, potatoes have been a critical part of the Irish diet. I read that the average Irish citizen eats nearly 190 pounds of potatoes per year, so it's still a very important crop today.

Mr. O'Leary took off his hat and scratched his head.

Gannon walked over, covered head to toe in manure.

"Top of the mornin' to ya?" he said, making a poor attempt at an Irish accent.

Mr. O'Leary just grumbled and continued to survey the crops.

"What's the matter?" Gannon asked.

"Agh, my crops have gone from bad to worse," he said. "These here will need to be dug up. Even more concerning, about half of my sheep have gone sick. Tried everything I know but can't seem to nurse them back to health."

"What do you think could be causing this?" I asked.

"Hard to say these days. Soil could be bad. Could be something in the air or the water. I'm not sure, but I do have a hunch about it."

"What's your hunch?"

"I think it has something to do with Moloney's place."

"Who's Moloney?" Gannon asked.

"Big-shot businessman," he said. "Owns the Francis Bacon paintings you'll see tonight, and a large farm about five kilometers upriver. But I shouldn't even call it a farm. That's giving the place more credit than it deserves."

"What do you mean?"

"It's what they call a Concentrated Animal Feeding Operation. Basically a big factory that produces meat and poultry. It's no life for the animals, I'll tell you that. Horrid conditions. They're kept in tight quarters, can't graze, and they're filled with all kinds of hormones and antibiotics. Makes the animals grow faster, but it's not the way nature intended, that's for certain. Personally, I wouldn't touch a single bite of the meat that comes out of that place."

"I've heard about this type of farm in the U.S.," Gannon said.

"Sadly, it's the new way of doing business," Mr. O'Leary said. "It's all about maximizing profit. They don't care about the animals. Don't care about the pollution or how unhealthy the meat is to the people who eat it. It's money, lads. Money is all they're after."

"So how is Moloney's place hurting your farm?" I asked.

"He's polluting the countryside! Used to be trout bigger than my arm in this river here. These days, I can hardly catch a thing. I see more dead fish than living. My guess is that the factory runoff and chemicals pumped into the air from his operations are doing serious damage to the environment. Problem is, I can't prove it. Had the county commissioners up there to run some tests and they say it all checks out. Personally, I think Moloney's got them in his back pocket."

"You mean he's paying off the commissioners?" Gannon asked.

"Unfortunate it is, lad, but these things sometimes happen," Mr. O'Leary said.

I perked up, realizing this was a perfect opportunity to put my knowledge of science to good use.

"Mr. O'Leary, I think I can help," I said.

"How's that?"

"Gannon and I could hike upriver and run some tests on the water near his farm. With the equipment I have in my backpack, I can test for chemical toxicity, bacteria, and all kinds of other pollutants. These tests will tell us exactly what's in the water. I can also run tests to see what's in the air. Maybe our results would force the county commissioners to take action and make Mr. Moloney clean up his operation."

"I like the idea, lad," he said, running his fingers over his stubbly cheeks. "We have the right to know the truth, but this is dangerous business you're considering here. Moloney plays hardball. One of his goons catches you up there and you could find yourself in a real scrape."

"But it seems pretty obvious that he's polluting," Gannon said. "And if we don't do something to stop him, it'll only get worse. It could destroy your farm, and farms all over the county. We can't let him do that!"

"We'll stay out of sight," I said. "Trust us, we're good at that."

Mr. O'Leary took off his cap and scratched his head.

"In good conscience, I can't put you lads in harm's way," he said. "If I tell you to do it and you get nabbed, I don't know that I'll be able to do anything to help you out. Let's just leave it alone for now."

"But, Mr. O'Leary . . ." Gannon said.

"That's the end of it, lads. He catches you and you'll wish you'd never come to Ireland, trust me on that. I'll work this out some other way. Now, get back to work, you hear me?"

"Yes, sir," I said, disappointed.

I understand Mr. O'Leary's concerns, but I can't see why he won't let us test the water and air near the factory farm. It's not like Mr. Moloney owns the river or the air. They belong to the people of Ireland, so it's our right to take samples, as far as I'm concerned.

From what I gather, Kilgore Moloney seems like a real villainous character, willing to do whatever it takes to protect his business. But what are the chances we'd get caught? I don't want to disobey Mr. O'Leary's wishes, but it's going to be hard to keep my curiosity from getting the best of me.

PART II

A QUEST FOR TRUTH

GANNON

We're off to Dromoland Castle shortly, and I'm dressed to the nines and looking pretty dapper, if I do say so myself. My hair is meticulously combed and parted on the left side, and I'm wearing my black suit which I always bring with me, just in case—a white oxford, a bright red tie, and a pair of freshly polished wingtips. I even stuffed a little red handkerchief into my coat pocket to match my tie. I mean, if you can't get away with being fancy at a castle, when can you?

Earlier, I slipped into the O'Learys' reading room, which, without question, is my favorite room in the house. There are bookshelves covering the walls on three sides, each packed tight with books from one end to the other. Every corner of the room has a comfortable reading chair and a small table with a lamp. There's also a fireplace with a few family photos on the mantel, including a beautiful portrait of Grace's mom. The whole room smells of freshly burnt peat logs, which is what the Irish typically use instead of wood. The logs are cut right out of the marshy bogs and have a distinct turf-like smell that I've really grown to like.

Peat logs being cut from the bog

Browsing the shelves, I came across a big section of art books. There were books on Michelangelo, Monet, Cezanne, Van Gogh, Picasso, Warhol, and a bunch of artists I'd never heard of. After flipping through a couple of them, I noticed a book on Francis Bacon. Well, given that we were about to see his most famous work, I figured I should know a little bit about it.

"Three Studies of Lucian Freud" is made up of three canvases. Each is 78 x 52 inches, so, let's see, that's about 6 1/2 feet tall by 4 1/3 feet wide. Jeez, I guess whoever buys those babies is going to need a pretty big wall to display them. The distorted figure on each of the three canvases is Lucian Freud, obviously, but what I didn't know is that Lucian was a famous painter too, and a good friend of Francis Bacon. The paintings were created back in 1969 and are now considered an icon of twentieth-century art. Guess that goes without saying, given the price they're expected to sell for.

Okay, I can hear Mr. O'Leary outside packing up the truck, which means it's about time to hit the road. Dromoland Castle, here we come!

WYATT

OCTOBER 6, 9:40 PM
DROMOLAND CASTLE, 52° 47' N   8° 54' W
49° FAHRENHEIT, 9° CELSIUS
WIND 15-20 MPH, RAIN

Pulling up the long driveway, raindrops pounded hard on Mr. O'Leary's truck. Windshield wipers whisked away the rain, giving way to momentary views of the property's manicured grounds. Finally, emerging from the trees that lined the road, Dromoland Castle came into view.

The castle was even bigger than I expected, probably the size of a soccer field, with high walls of gray stone, made darker by the drenching rains. Ivy grew on the walls in parts, covering everything but the windows. It looked as much like a fortress as a castle, built to protect its inhabitants from invasion and ferocious weather. Atop the highest tower, an Irish flag whipped back and forth in the blustery winds.

We drove around to the front of the castle, and Mr. O'Leary came to a stop at the steps.

Dromoland Castle, County Clare

"Da, are you sure you can't join us?" Grace asked before she got out of the truck.

"No, have to tend to the tractor," he said. "Besides, I don't think I could stomach being in the same room as that wretched Kilgore Moloney."

"Be nice, Da," Grace said. "If it weren't for him, we wouldn't have the pleasure of seeing these remarkable paintings. Technically, we're his guests, you know?"

"I know. Doesn't mean I have to like him, though. Now get going, kids. I need to get the tractor to Galway before it gets too late."

Grace kissed her father on the cheek, Gannon and I thanked him, and we all raced up the steps toward the castle.

Two giant doors, at least six inches thick and ten feet high, swung open and the sound of bagpipes met us as we entered. Just inside the door stood a man dressed in a tuxedo.

"Grace, my dear," the man said.

Grace immediately hugged him.

"How are you this evening?" he asked.

"A little wet, but otherwise wonderful," she said. "We're certainly having some weather, aren't we?"

"We sure are," Gannon said.

"Martin, I'd like you to meet my new friends, Gannon and Wyatt."

"Ah yes," he said. "The young lads who are working on your farm."

"That's right," I said and shook Martin's hand. "I'm Wyatt."

"Wyatt, it is a pleasure," he said.

I don't know if it's nerves or what, but Gannon often has difficulty acting appropriate in formal situations. I was hoping tonight wouldn't be one of those occasions, but right away I knew he wasn't going to be able to help himself.

"Bring it up high," Gannon said, raising his hand for a high-five.

Martin looked confused.

"Come on," Gannon said, still holding up his hand. "Up top."

Reluctantly, Martin raised his white glove and patted Gannon's hand.

"Wow," Gannon said, looking around the castle, "not too shabby. Not too shabby at all."

"Quite right, sir." Martin said.

"Oh, come on, Martin. Do I look like a sir to you? Please, call me Gannon."

"Yes, sir. Mr. Gannon," Martin said, a little flustered. "Welcome to Dromoland Castle."

We followed Martin into an elaborate gathering room. Directly ahead of us, two suits of armor stood guard, each holding a knight's sword. Brown leather reading chairs and couches lined the walls. Between the chairs were tables, each with a burning candle in the center. On one of the tables sat a chessboard. To the left was a wall of old hardcover books.

Ornately patterned curtains framed each of the windows, and several crystal chandeliers hung from the high ceiling.

A knight's suit of armor

"Looks like the kind of place where a ghost might take up residence," Gannon said, looking all around. "You think it's haunted? I'd bet you a hundred dollars it is."

I gave him a quick shot to the ribs.

"Jeez, what was that for?" Gannon asked.

"For opening your mouth. Please, do us all a favor and keep it shut while we're here."

"Why?" Gannon said.

"Because when you open it embarrassing words come flying out."

"Lighten up. I'm just having a little fun. Besides, I'm starting to feel especially talkative. I think the gift of gab is staring to kick in."

"I'm just warning you, don't make a fool out of yourself, okay? If you do, Mr. O'Leary's going to hear about it and that won't be good for either of us."

"Póg amach, Wyatt."

"You better tell me what that means."

"You're a smart guy. You'll figure it out eventually."

At that, Gannon straightened his tie and followed Grace deeper into the castle. I stayed close, weaving through the halls until we came to the main dining room. Rain drove sideways into the windows, producing a continuous clattering roar. An occasional rumble of thunder rattled an enormous chandelier overhead. I made a mental note not to walk directly underneath it, just in case.

Martin quietly pointed out some of the guests, which included the who's who of art collectors. There were members of the Irish Parliament, a prince and countess, and a handful of foreign dignitaries. Other guests included a Las Vegas casino owner, several recognizable Hollywood actors, and renowned artists from New York, Paris, Florence, and

Berlin. We even saw the lead singer of Ireland's most famous rock band, U2.

"Where the streets have no name, baby!" Gannon shouted across the room when he saw him. "I love that song! It's one of my faves!"

If I'd been closer to Gannon I would have given him another shot to the ribs, this time much harder.

Tuxedoed waiters served drinks in Waterford crystal and presented hors d'oeuvres on silver trays. In the dining room stood a life-sized ice sculpture of a red deer with an impressive set of antlers. Everyone in the castle was dressed in suits and ball gowns. Some of the older gentlemen carried canes and wore top hats.

I made my way into the grand ballroom where the paintings were on display. On a large white wall bathed in overhead light hung three canvases that commanded your attention. Each canvas had a bright yellow background, the color of the afternoon sun. In the center of each was a strange, disfigured man. It reminded me of what a person might look like to someone suffering from double vision. The paintings were peculiar, to say the least. But what do I know? For whatever reason, art doesn't register with me. I guess I just don't get it. So, to be fair to Mr. Bacon, most art seems peculiar to me.

Of course, Gannon thinks he's some kind of art critic. I couldn't help but roll my eyes when I saw him standing in the center of the room, rubbing his chin as he stared intensely at the paintings.

I walked up behind him.

"Would you like to hear my interpretation of this work?" he asked without diverting his eyes from the paintings.

"No thanks," I said.

"In my opinion," he continued, "this work is an exploration of emotional and physical expressionism. Notice the distorted human form. It captures the essence of what the expressionist painters were going for during this period. It's truly remarkable on all accounts. The crowning achievement in the triumphant career of an artistic genius."

"Did you eat some bad oysters or something?" I asked. "Seriously, where did you come up with that jibberish?"

"Read it in a book at the O'Leary's," he said.

A waiter approached.

"Pesto shrimp and avocado crostini?" he said, holding out a silver tray lined with bite-sized appetizers.

"Don't mind if I do," Gannon said, and popped one in his mouth.

"How are they, sir?" the waiter asked.

"Mmm," Gannon said, grabbed two more, and tossed them both into his mouth while still chewing the first. "They're divine."

"Don't talk with your mouth full," I said.

"But these are so good. You gotta try one."

I walked away, deciding it was best to keep my distance the rest of the night. I reasoned that as long as I couldn't hear my brother talk he wouldn't be able to annoy me.

Oh, was I wrong. Just thinking ahead to what happened next stresses me out all over again. I'm sure that if I start to write about it in my journal my blood pressure will shoot through the roof, and if that happens it's likely I won't be able to fall asleep, and if that happens tomorrow's work on the farm will be a real struggle. It's probably best I close my journal, turn off the lamp, and attempt the impossible task of forgetting about tonight's disaster.

GANNON

OCTOBER 7
FEELING THE NEED TO DEFEND MY
ACTIONS AT DROMOLAND CASTLE

Let me start by saying that when I have something on my mind, someone, somewhere is usually going to hear about it. In some situations this habit of mine isn't any big deal. People can just ignore me or plug their ears or whatever. In other situations, I'll admit, it can cause a bit of a problem.

Let me give a "for instance."

So, I'm gazing up at "Three Studies of Lucian Freud," giving Wyatt a scholarly interpretation of the work, when a hush came over the ballroom.

"There he is," a woman whispered.

There who is, I wondered and turned to see a tall, lean man with a translucent face standing in the entryway.

Leaning over, I whispered to the woman, "And who might he be?"

"The owner of the paintings," she said. "Kilgore Artemis Moloney."

Okay, if I were to imagine a bright, jolly, teddy bear of a man, the kind of gent who'd hand out lollipops to kids, and then, you know, imagine the total opposite, well, that'd be Kilgore Moloney.

No joke, the guy gave me the heebie-jeebies. He's got this thick, black hair that's slicked straight back, and this eerily chiseled face that's as pale as a corpse, with round cheek-bones and a pointy nose, and, oh man, these dark, piercing eyes that look like they could burn a hole right through you. He was wearing a three-piece suit, black as midnight, with a shiny gold pocket watch dangling from his vest.

Standing just behind him was a hulk of a man, three times the width of Mr. Moloney and bright with color in comparison. His hair was brownish-red, his eyes vivid green, and his plump cheeks a rosy shade of pink. He was wearing a navy blue pinstriped suit, which, because of his girth, looked as if it was about to blow out at the seams.

"Please, be sure to take one last look at these treasured paintings," Mr. Moloney said to the crowd. "After the auc-tion, what the new owner decides to do with these works of art is not of my concern, but it is likely they will not be exhibited to the public again for some time."

"Mr. Moloney!" a man shouted from the crowd. "After

you sell the paintings what are you going to do with all the money?"

"That is a good question," he replied. "I have plans to expand my largest enterprise, the Moloney Factory Farm Complex."

People turned to one another and began commenting quietly.

"Investing the profit I make from the paintings into my farming enterprise, we expect our output will grow to twenty times what it is today, making the Moloney Factory Farm Complex the largest livestock operation in all of Europe."

Oh man, I did not like that sound of Mr. Moloney's plans. Not one bit. Twenty times bigger? That just meant twenty times the pollution. Shamrock Farm wouldn't stand a chance. Heck, every family farm in the county would be in trouble.

As usual, I couldn't keep my thoughts to myself.

"Mr. Moloney," I said, just loud enough to be heard from the back of the ballroom, "If I may?"

The crowd parted, putting me in direct view of Mr. Moloney. He stared at me coldly, his dark eyes so frightening they nearly turned me to stone. Finally, he nodded his head, inviting my comments. I gulped down my fear and stepped forward.

"With all due respect, sir," I said. "The whole thing about expanding your factory farm and all, well, I'm sorry, but I don't think it's a very good idea."

"Young man," Mr. Moloney said, "how could you say that producing more food for more people isn't a good idea? The world's population is increasing at an alarming rate. Every year there are millions more mouths to feed. Global food production struggles to keep up. Would you suggest we allow more people to go hungry?"

"No, it's not that," I said. "I mean, feeding more people, obviously that's a great thing."

"Then what is it, lad?"

"It's just the way you go about it at your farm."

"The way I go about it?" he repeated with a scowl.

"Yeah, I mean, from what I've been told by some pretty reliable sources, factory farms don't use the best practices."

Out of the corner of my eye, I could see Wyatt pushing people aside to get to me. I noticed Martin doing the same from the other end of the room. I knew I didn't have much time.

"Again, with all due respect, factory farms like yours, sir, they do harm to the environment. They spew toxic chemicals into the air we breathe and contaminate the water we drink. And the way the animals are treated, well, it's . . ." I was searching for the right words. All of a sudden, several popped into my head. "It's inhuman, unethical, and just plain wrong. No animal deserves to live the way they do in a factory farm."

"These animals feed people," he said. "That is their purpose."

"Well, what about the beef that comes out of your place?

It probably has enough hormones and harmful antibiotics in it to make people sick. Am I right?"

Mr. Moloney turned to the people nearest to him.

"This young man is talking complete rubbish," I heard him say.

Wyatt made his way to me and squeezed my arm hard. His face was as red as an apple.

"Have you lost your mind?" he whispered through clenched teeth.

"Don't distract me," I whispered. "I'm getting to my point."

"Forget your point. Nobody wants to hear it. Shut your mouth now, or I'll shut it for you."

Mr. Moloney addressed the crowd.

"I will have you all know that the beef we export from Ireland feeds nearly 30 million people around the world, 2.5 million of whom I feed personally with the meat I export from my farm complex. After the expansion, I will feed many more."

The crowd applauded.

I began to panic.

I'd started a debate, and I was losing.

"But there are better ways to go about feeding more people," I said. "Ways that are better for the local family farms. Better for the consumers who eat your meat. Better for the environment. Let me give you an example . . ."

Before I could say another word, someone grabbed me by

the shoulders and jerked me backward. A massive hand came over my face, cupping my mouth, nose, and eyes all at once. Everything went black, like a total eclipse. I could hardly breathe. I was being pulled out of the room and fought hopelessly to break free.

When that giant hand finally peeled away I gasped for breath. There was chaos all around me. Wyatt, Martin, Grace, and Mr. Moloney's bodyguard were all yelling at one another.

"You escort him out of the castle or I'll do it for you!" the bodyguard shouted at Martin. "And trust me, the young lad won't enjoy that too much!"

"I will take care of it," Martin said.

At that, the bodyguard stormed off.

Martin took my arm and ushered me to the front of the castle.

"My dad's going to have a fit," Grace said as we walked quickly down the hall. "He's no fan of Mr. Moloney, but there is a time and place to make your opinions heard, and this was not the time nor the place."

Okay, I'll admit, maybe my rant was a little out of line given the setting and all, but at the same time I knew in my heart that I was right. Still, hearing the anger in Grace's voice, oh man, it made me feel terrible.

"Maybe I shouldn't have kissed the Blarney Stone," I whispered to Wyatt, attempting to lighten the mood.

"Are you sure you didn't kiss the Idiot Stone?" he shouted

back. He was pacing, running his fingers through his hair. "I know you're my twin brother, but I'm not taking a single ounce of blame for this. The thoughts and opinions expressed inappropriately at this event are that of the moronic speaker and have nothing to do with his far more intelligent sibling."

"I think it's best we conclude the evening," Martin said. "Besides, I promised Mr. O'Leary I would take you back to the farm at a reasonable hour, and I believe now is a reasonable hour. If you will, please follow me to the car."

Martin led us through the doors back into the rain. Grace walked at least ten feet ahead and wouldn't even make eye contact with me. As we approached the car, Martin put his hand on my shoulder.

"I suggest that tomorrow you formally apologize to Mr. O'Leary," he said. "Might help improve things a tad."

"That's good advice, Martin," I said. "I think I'll do that."

Grace wouldn't speak to me the rest of the night, which left me with this real queasy feeling in my stomach. I'd honestly do anything to get myself back in good standing with her.

I mean it when I say that I'm really sorry for embarrassing Grace and Mr. O'Leary. And I understand that what I did was out-of-line and inappropriate and should have been handled differently and all that. But, come on! Somebody has to speak up, right? Kilgore Moloncy is using Ireland's rivers, lakes, and air as his own personal waste dump. Mr. O'Leary said it himself. I mean, hello! Is everyone really okay with this? I can't imagine that anyone is, but for whatever reason, no one seems to have the courage to stand up to this guy.

Personally, I'm pretty far from okay with it. I mean, just thinking about it is making me crazy all over again. Plus, I haven't had breakfast yet this morning, which is making me even crankier. Okay, I need to eat and get to work. If Wyatt hasn't decided to completely ignore me, maybe we can talk things over and come up with a plan.

WYATT

OCTOBER 7, 12:47 PM
SHAMROCK FARM
56° FAHRENHEIT, 13° CELSIUS
WIND 5-10 MPH, PARTLY SUNNY

Farmland on the Emerald Isle

Early this morning the clouds parted, allowing the sun to embrace the land for the first time since we arrived at the farm. The air outside was crisp and smelled of pine. Everything was bright green, almost glowing. Even the birds were happy, chirping away in the trees.

Despite the near perfect weather, Gannon's episode at the castle hung over us like a dark cloud. Walking to the barn to gather some tools, I found him sprawled out in a pile of hay.

"What are you doing?" I asked.

"Just polished off a Full-Irish," Gannon said. "I'm so stuffed I can hardly move."

A "Full-Irish," as it's known in the country, is a hearty breakfast that includes bacon, sausage, eggs, potatoes, blood pudding, buttered toast, and grilled tomatoes.

"I'm surprised you even had an appetite after what you pulled last night."

"Hey, we both know Mr. O'Leary's going to bring down the hammer when he hears about it. I figured I'd handle it a little better on a full stomach. You know, as opposed to an empty one."

"Sometimes it's hard for me to believe we're actually related."

"Lay off, would you? I admit I probably didn't go about it the way I should have, but it needed to be said. Obviously, I was the only one who had the guts to say it."

"Just get up already," I said, kicking his leg. "It's time to get to work. Mr. O'Leary comes home and finds you lying around in the hay, it's going to be twice as bad for you."

Gannon finally sat up.

"Fine," he said. "Have you seen Grace yet this morning?"

"No, I haven't."

"Man, I hate the thought of her being mad at me. I hope I can make it up to her somehow."

"Don't hold your breath on that one."

We loaded our tools into the wheelbarrow and walked from the barn.

As we made our way toward the field, Mr. O'Leary's truck came flying down the driveway. It slid to a stop in front of the house, and Mr. O'Leary jumped out, waving a newspaper around in his hand.

"Now there's nothing we can do to stop that fool!" Mr. O'Leary shouted. "He has all the money in the world!"

Grace stepped out of the house to see what all the shouting was about. Gannon and I met them on the porch.

"What's the matter, Da?" Grace said.

"See for yourself!" he said and slammed the paper down on the porch table.

The headline read: "Francis Bacon Paintings Fetch Record Price at Auction!"

"Read the first column," Mr. O'Leary said with a huff. "Spells it all out in black and white."

I picked up the paper and read the first column aloud:

Francis Bacon's "Three Studies of Lucian Freud" sold at last night's auction for a record $144 million, the highest price ever paid for a work of art. The buyer, American businesswoman Margaret Sorenson, plans to include the paintings in her private collection, which is currently housed in her Greek-themed Las Vegas casino, the Acropolis. The event at Dromoland Castle was ripe with drama, beginning with the expulsion of a young man protesting the proposed expansion of the Moloney Factory Farm Complex. The planned development, according to Kilgore Moloney, would increase the size and capacity of the farm complex by twenty times, making it the largest such operation in Europe. Moloney apologized to guests for the young man's outburst and assured everyone that it would take much more than the misguided mumblings of a teenager to stop the expansion from moving forward.

I dropped the paper.

Everyone glared at Gannon.

"Yeah, about that . . ." Gannon said.

"Agh," Mr. O'Leary said, swatting his hand in the air. "Normally I'd rake you over the coals for such a foolish stunt, and don't get me wrong, I'm furious that you'd go and embarrass my Gracie like that. You were her guest. Blimey, lad! I can't help but wonder, do you have any sense of when to keep your mouth shut?"

"That's the thing," Gannon said. "I really don't."

"So it seems," said Mr. O'Leary.

"I'm so sorry, Grace," Gannon said. "Honest, the last thing I meant to do was embarrass you."

"It's okay, Gannon," she said in a sweet voice. "I'll get over it."

"Phew, am I relieved to hear that," he said.

"Given what Moloney is doing with the profits from the paintings, part of me admires your effort," Mr. O'Leary said.

"Wow, so relieved to hear that too," Gannon said, wiping his brow with his sleeve.

"Fact of the matter is, we don't stand much of a chance. This farm has been around for six generations. It survived the great famine. But this very well could be the end of it."

"Don't say that, Da," Grace said. "There has to be a way to keep the farm going."

"We can't compete with a massive operation like Moloney's. And even if we could, the pollution from that treacherous place is already destroying our farm! Multiply that times twenty and nothing will be able to survive! Shamrock Farm will become a barren wasteland!"

Mr. O'Leary picked up the paper and flung it into the air.

"I'm taking the day to figure out what we do next!" he said, storming off the porch. "I'm in no mood to talk about it anymore, so please let me be!"

"Mr. O'Leary," I said timidly. "Don't you want us to work in the fields today?"

"Why bother?" he shouted and disappeared around the corner of the barn.

Grace has gone off to try to calm her father. Gannon and I have retreated to the guest room, still trying to come to terms with Mr. O'Leary's bleak outlook on the future of the family farm. For all intents and purposes, he feels that it's all over for them. And the sad truth is, he might be right.

GANNON

This whole throwing in the towel attitude just doesn't fly with me. Okay, sure, the situation is not good. But as far as I'm concerned, the fate of Shamrock Farm is far from a done deal. We just need to take action, so that's what we're doing.

"This is ridiculous, us sitting around like two bumps on a log," I said to Wyatt, breaking a long silence. "It's time to make a move."

"What do you have in mind?" Wyatt asked.

"How about we sneak off and gather some water and air samples around Moloney's complex? You and I both know he is polluting big-time. Wouldn't you love to be the one who nails him for it? If we can prove that it's as bad as Mr. O'Leary says it is, the county would have to shut him down, right?"

"I would think so," Wyatt said.

"Then I don't see that we have a choice."

"I agree," Wyatt said, "but Mr. O'Leary told us to stay out of it. You heard him yourself. If we go snooping around Moloney's, we could get ourselves into serious trouble."

"That's a risk I'm willing to take," I said. "Come on, you with me?"

"I don't know," Wyatt said, turning away.

Luckily, I know how to persuade my brother. Little trick I've used about a thousand times. It's called "stroking his ego."

"I can't do it without you, Wyatt," I said. "When it comes to scientific mumbo-jumbo, I don't have a clue what I'm doing. You're the one with the knowledge. You know how to take samples and how to make heads or tails of the results. Let's face it, bro, you're the smart one."

"I'm still listening," Wyatt said, rubbing his chin.

"Without you, this mission is hopeless. If you won't do it for me, do it for the O'Learys. With your help, we might be able to save their farm."

Wyatt looked out the window. Up on the hill stood the towering Scots pine, a beautiful reminder of the family history on this land.

"Okay," Wyatt said. "I'm in. Let's do it."

"All righty then!" I shouted. "Let's prove to everyone that the factory farm is doing some harm!"

"Right, got it."

Wyatt began loading his backpack, but I was on a roll.

"Here's a better one," I said. "Let's prove that Mr. Moloney is full of baloney!"

"Seriously, that's enough."

"One more. Let's go tell the polluters that they can't . . . uh . . . shoot, I can't think of anything that rhymes with polluters."

"And just when I thought the Blarney Stone might have *actually* given you the gift of gab," he said.

"It's going to happen one of these days. You watch."

Okay, we're packed and just about ready to roll. Wyatt and I already explained our plan to Grace. At first she didn't want us to disobey her father's wishes, and I totally get that, but after hearing us out she finally agreed that it's more important to know the truth. Grace sketched out a map and outlined a shortcut to Moloney's Farm Complex. It takes us off the path of the river, directly over the ridge, and will get us there in about an hour, if we don't get lost. Once Wyatt finishes checking his equipment, our mission begins!

WYATT

OCTOBER 7, 3:51 PM
OUTSIDE MOLONEY'S FACTORY FARM COMPLEX
53° FAHRENHEIT, 12° CELSIUS
WIND 10-20 MPH, RAIN

Following well-drawn directions from Grace, we came to forested hilltop spotted with boulders. Wind blew fiercely up the slopes of the hill, whipping the tree limbs into a frenzy.

Dark clouds moved through the sky. Another storm was coming off the North Atlantic.

Scrambling over the moss-covered boulders, the forest opened up into a massive area of land where the trees had been clear-cut. There before us in the valley stood an enormous complex. If I had not already known of its existence and general location, I would never have been able to guess this was any type of farm. It looked more like an industrial compound, made up of a series of giant warehouses, each with a towering chimney spewing plumes of gray smoke that eventually fused with the stormy sky. There were five warehouse buildings in total, each the size of a football field. At the far end of the warehouses, along the banks of the river, were two rectangular-shaped ponds, pea-green in color. Waste ponds are what they were. Basically, holes in the ground where all the animals' waste was stored. I couldn't believe how close they were to the river—a river that provides fresh water for hundreds of local farmers, not to mention hundreds of thousands of Irish citizens. The entire complex was surrounded by a thick concrete wall.

The darkest clouds moved east and the wind subsided. Ashy soot tumbled like snowflakes from the sky, landing on the sleeves of my raincoat. The distant sounds of the farm suddenly met our ears, the mingled cries of thousands of animals—cows, pigs, chickens, sheep—I could only describe it as disturbing.

"Mr. Moloney's farm, I'm guessing?" Gannon asked.

"I think so."

"It's even worse than I thought."

Moloney's farm complex was a big operation as is. With plans to expand it to twenty times its current size, there would be one hundred warehouses and forty waste ponds. The environmental damage we could see from the hillside was already bad enough. We didn't even need to run tests to see that he was polluting the air, water, and land. It was obvious. Multiply this damage times twenty, and it would be disastrous.

"That's the river that flows right through Shamrock Farm," I said. "I bet Mr. O'Leary is right. The pollution from this factory is what's killing his crops and making his live-stock sick."

"Uh, you think?"

"Let's get closer to the factory so I can take some water samples."

I took a few photographs as we moved closer, navigating slippery rocks and muddy slopes, all the way to the complex wall, which was at least twice our height.

"Should we scale it?" I asked. "We really need water sam-ples from the section of the river closest to the waste ponds. That will show exactly what contaminants he's dumping into the water system, and how much."

"I'm all for scaling it," Gannon said. "You have no idea how badly I want to bust this guy. Give me a boost. I'll pull myself up and then give you a hand. And let's be quick about it."

If we were spotted, I knew we'd be in a world of trouble, so we scaled the wall as fast as we could and did our best to stay out of sight, even crawling on our stomachs down to the riverbank.

"Wow, that's some serious stink," Gannon said. "Reminds me of you after a couple days of camping."

I ignored him and pulled my shirt up over my nose. The stench of the waste was almost too much to tolerate. Below the waste ponds, there were small tributaries of green muck running down the hillside into the river. I took several pictures as proof that they were dumping the waste into the river illegally. Gannon stayed hidden behind some rocks to keep a look out and take some video.

Once I was directly below the waste ponds, I crawled up to the beachhead and filled a small bottle with river water. Fact is, it wasn't water at all, but a thick sludge so putrid I gagged as I capped the bottle. Moloney's dumping had turned this pristine river into a waste slick. The smooth river stones were coated like there had been an oil spill.

After making my way further downriver, close to the far border of Moloney's property, I filled a second bottle and then crept back up the hill to Gannon's lookout.

I was ready to leave the complex, but Gannon wasn't satisfied.

"We need to get inside one of these warehouses," he said.

"Why would we want to do that? We have plenty of evidence already."

"What about the animals? I want to document their living conditions on video. I bet it's awful in there, but I need proof."

"It's too risky to go inside. I'm afraid we'll get caught."

"Moloney's a powerful man. If we really want to stop him, we have to gather as much evidence as possible."

I needed some time to think this all through, but as usual, Gannon was being very impatient.

"We've come this far, Wyatt. I'm not leaving before I see the animals. So, you coming or not?"

"All right. But if we get caught, I'm telling Mom and Dad this was all your idea."

"Fine. Let's go."

We made our way down the hill and carefully crossed the river just above the waste ponds where the water was cleaner. Just up the bank was the nearest warehouse. Through a metal door on the side of the building, we could hear the squeals of what sounded like thousands of pigs. The door was locked, but a small window gave us a peek inside. Unfortunately, a high wall of shelving lined with tools and machinery obscured our view.

Continuing around the back of the building we found another door, but it was locked too. Then we heard a loud ratcheting sound and saw that one of the garage doors was opening. Gannon and I ran and dove behind a forklift parked near the garage. Inside, we heard an engine come to life. Moments later a flat bed semitruck drove through the garage door. Cages were stacked twenty feet high on the bed of the truck from one end to the other. Inside these cages were hundreds of piglets. They looked no more than a few weeks old and were squealing like mad, probably scared half to death after being taken away from their mothers.

"Quick, this is our chance," Gannon said as the truck passed.

We ran for the garage door and rolled underneath just before it closed. Inside, we found cover behind a stack of wooden crates. The stench inside was nauseating, and we both pulled our shirts over our noses.

"Ready to collect some more evidence?" Gannon asked as he prepped his video camera.

"Ready," I said.

"Good. Get as many photos as you can. It won't be long before someone notices us."

When we stood up and looked across the warehouse neither of us could believe our eyes. As far as we could see were rows of metal cages and inside each was a pig. There were literally thousands of them. Each cage was just big enough for the pig to fit inside. They were so confining, the pigs couldn't even turn around.

I snapped off dozens of photos while Gannon took some video.

"This is so upsetting," I said.

"Pigs are intelligent animals," Gannon said. "Can you imagine what they must be feeling? I mean, they're forced to live in these tiny cages and then have their babies taken away from them. It's so sad."

"Like Mr. O'Leary said, it's definitely not the way nature intended."

"Oh, shoot," Gannon said, pulling me down. "Someone's coming."

I peered between the crates. About twenty men wearing gas masks and protective yellow suits came into the warehouse, each one holding what looked like a shiny silver gun. The masked men lined up at the far end of the warehouse and systematically marched forward, using the guns to inject something into the hindquarter of each pig. I assumed it was an antibiotic to keep them from getting sick, or some kind of growth hormone to make them grow faster. Whatever it was, the injections caused the pigs to squeal and jerk away violently, smashing themselves hard into metal bars.

Careful to stay out of sight, I managed to get some close-up photographs of the men as they administered the shots to the pigs. But they were moving our way in a hurry, so we had to make a break for it.

Crawling across the ground, we made it out the back door and sprinted away like we were running for our lives. After crossing the river and scaling the wall, we climbed to the ridge that overlooks the complex and stopped to catch our breath. I scanned the complex grounds to see if anyone was following us.

"Doesn't look like we were spotted," I said.

"Oh man, the sound of those pigs squealing," Gannon said, panting. "I just can't get it out of my head. It was haunting."

"It's ringing in my ears too."

"And we only saw one of the warehouses. Grace said he has cows, chickens, and sheep, too. And I guarantee they aren't treated any better. I mean, it's kind of mind-boggling that an operation like this can even exist."

"Remember what Mr. O'Leary said. Moloney has no problem bribing officials to look the other way."

"Well, with the evidence we just collected, they won't be able to look the other way much longer. I think our case will be strong enough to get this place closed down. If the county officials are all being paid off, we'll take it right to Ireland's Environmental Protection Agency, Parliament, the prime minister. I'm not joking. After seeing what we just saw, winning this battle is the only option!"

Gannon was right. Now that we know the gruesome extent of Moloney's polluting and his hideous treatment of the animals, we have to put a stop to it.

I was anxious to test the samples I'd taken, so I set up my water and air testing equipment right on the rocks. Gannon watched the video and scrolled through the photos as I worked to obtain some initial results.

They were even worse than I expected.

"Nitrate levels are off the charts," I said. "And there's all kinds of pathogens in the water. There's cryptosporidium, for starters, and the air around this complex shows high levels of hydrogen sulfide, most likely from the pigs."

"Sounds bad," Gannon said, "but I honestly don't have a clue what any of it means."

"Basically, these contaminants could severely impact a person's health over time. Too much exposure could even cause death."

"Wait a sec. So you're saying the pollution coming from that place over there is bad enough to kill people?"

"It's scary but true."

"Jeez, if I had the power, I'd lock Moloney up in a cell and throw the key into that nasty waste pond."

I noticed the daylight was fading fast.

"It'll be dark soon," I said. "We better find a place to stay for the night."

I carefully loaded the equipment into my backpack and we set out. A little farther along the ridge, we found a shelter among the rocks that was dry and upwind from Moloney's farm complex and decided it was a good place to settle until morning. We hadn't planned to stay out overnight, but trying to navigate the forest in the dark would not be a wise decision. We've been lost in a forest before and would prefer not to have that experience again.

GANNON

Okay, I need to make some quick notes in my journal while I have the chance. Additional evidence not only of the crimes being committed but of Moloney's knowledge of it all. Basically, he's aware of the damage he's doing but keeps right on doing it anyway. This morning I got proof.

Just as the sun came up, I heard voices across the river.

"Wyatt," I whispered. "I think someone's coming."

"Let's get out of here," he said. "Stay low."

We grabbed our backpacks and slithered out of the cave, moving down the hillside toward the bushes along the river's edge. We were hidden but became trapped as three people walked down to the wide riverbank just outside the high gates of Moloney's complex. If we moved, they would see us!

"Stay still," I told Wyatt.

It was Mr. Moloney, his big, burly bodyguard, and a third man who was wearing a white smock. They were all looking into the river. Still as statues, we sat behind the bushes, listening to the men talk. Their voices carried clearly over the water.

"You can smell it distinctly when the wind shifts," the man wearing the smock said.

There was definitely a strong, rotten scent along the river. Different from the smell of the waste closer to the factory.

"I don't see anything," Mr. Moloney said, still peering into the river. "I think your claim is malarkey."

The man in the smock waded into the river, dragging a net through the water as he moved upstream. When he stepped back onto the bank, there was a fish in his net. He pulled a surgical mask up over his nose and mouth. So did Mr. Moloney's bodyguard. Mr. Moloney didn't. He just stood there with an evil scowl on his face.

"You see," the man said, showing Moloney the limp fish. "I believe the runoff from the waste ponds is killing them."

"That's just a guess!" Mr. Moloney shouted. "You don't know for sure! This fish could have died from any number of things!"

"There are more dead fish in this river, I assure you," the man said. "Lots more. We will run an autopsy just to be certain, but I'm quite sure it will prove what I say is true."

"No tests will be run, do you understand?" Mr. Moloney shouted. "That is an order! The county's environmental commissioner tested the water last year and gave it a clean bill! Why on earth would we run more tests? Besides, what do I care of a few dead fish? I am not in the business of fish! I am only concerned with the livestock at my complex. More specifically the amount of profit each head of livestock brings me. It has been determined that the cheapest and most efficient way to rid the farm of the waste is to release it into the river. It won't do any harm. Nature is durable, quick to bounce back, so I have no concern whatsoever. Any variation to my orders will result in your dismissal, do you understand?"

In defiance, the man in the smock turned his back on Mr. Moloney.

"Never turn your back on me," Mr. Moloney said coldly.

Reluctantly, the man turned around to face him.

"Tell me, Mr. Kipling," Mr. Moloney continued. "Are you married?"

"Yes, sir. I am."

"And do you have any children?"

"I have two daughters and a son."

"I don't suppose they would fare well with a father who no longer has the privilege of an income."

"No, sir. They would not."

"And if any word of this were to leak to the press, unemployment will be the least of your problems. Do I make myself clear?"

"Yes, sir."

"Then I suggest we get back to work. Let nature sort out the dead fish. It is none of my concern."

They all started back toward the factory.

"That man is just plain evil," I whispered. "He treats people almost as poorly as he treats animals."

"We have to get out of here," Wyatt said. "We have all the evidence we need. The only thing that could ruin our plan now is getting caught. Stay low and follow me."

And this is where we ran into a slight problem.

Making the goofball mistake of planting my foot on the slickest part of the rock, my legs went flying out from under me and I tumbled down the slope to the shoreline, crashing through all kinds of bushes along the way. Having totally knocked the wind out of myself, I sat up slowly, my eyes closed, and took a few long, deep breaths, trying desperately to replace the air that had been ejected from my lungs on impact. When I opened my eyes again, all three men were staring at me from across the river.

Oh man, was I busted!

"Don't worry about me," I grunted, still trying to catch my breath. "I'll be fine. Please, go about your business."

"Get him!" Mr. Moloney yelled.

Next thing I know, that big hulk of a bodyguard is running through the river like a stampeding rhino! He had a full head of steam and this crazy rage in his eyes. Probably furious that he was having to chase me through the river in that fancy blue suit of his.

Well, I wasn't about to wait around and see what happened if he caught me, so I hightailed it up the slope and followed Wyatt back toward the cover of the forest. Stinging pains shot through my ribs and back as I hurdled rocks and fallen trees. Didn't matter though. I wasn't stopping for anything. Moloney's big goon followed us as far as his tree trunk–sized legs could carry him, but that kind of physique isn't suited for long treks through rugged terrain. Eventually, he had to stop to catch his breath.

"You can't escape, you little rats!" he shouted between gasps. "I swear, I'll cut your throats when I get my hands on you!"

I smacked Wyatt on the chest with the back of my hand.

"Let's make sure that doesn't happen. Come on."

I mean, wow, did we score big at Moloney's! Now, all we need to do is keep from getting captured, find our way out of this spooky forest, and get the evidence to someone in the county government who isn't being paid off by Moloney. Okay, sure. Easier said than done, but we're going to do our best to make it all happen and set things straight.

Right, so that's enough for now. We have to get going. The trek back to Shamrock Farm continues . . .

WYATT

OCTOBER 8, 4:18 PM
48° FAHRENHEIT, 8° CELSIUS
WIND 5 MPH, RAIN

In a forest like this, it's easy to get lost

After a short rest, we hiked on at a brisk pace, deeper and deeper into the forest. The hike was difficult, wet, and slippery with lots of rocks and steep hills. Each step required focus and effort.

"Stop," Gannon finally said, panting. "I'm . . . exhausted. Need . . . to . . . rest."

My legs were sore and cramping. Dehydration, I thought. Rain was falling steadily so I tore a large leaf from a nearby plant. Cupping the leaf I sat patiently as the water collected inside. Once a puddle had accumulated in the leaf, I tilted it back and let the cool water fall into my mouth. We did this until Gannon and I each drank a good amount of water and felt ready to continue our trek.

Only one small issue: We weren't sure which way to go.

"We should have found Shamrock Farm by now, don't you think?" Gannon asked. "I mean, how long have we been hiking?"

I looked at my explorer watch.

"About two hours. Give or take."

"And how long did it take us to get to Moloney's on the way there?"

"About an hour."

"So, we've been hiking twice as long on the way back as we did on the way there, and Shamrock Farm is still nowhere to be seen. That would lead me to believe that we're lost. Would I be correct in that assumption?"

"I think so."

All of a sudden, I heard what sounded like a growl.

"What was that?" I asked.

"It was my stomach," Gannon said. "We have to get some food. My tank's on empty."

"I know there are some berries or mosses in this forest that are edible."

"Unless you're one hundred percent sure something is

safe to eat, I'm not putting it in my mouth. Besides, I need some real food."

"Sorry, Gannon, but I don't think there's anywhere to get a Full-Irish out here."

Gannon looked around, scanning the dense forest that surrounded us on all sides.

"This place gives me the creeps," he said.

"It's just a forest."

"Just a forest? I don't think so. You know what kind of things live out here? Elves, banshees, leprechauns. Probably all of the above."

"You've been reading too many fairy tales."

Just then Gannon pointed to the ground ahead of us.

"Speaking of fairies, look!"

Among the sprouts of grass was a circular formation of small rocks and pink rhododendrons. The flowers had been plucked and placed in a perfect circle. It seemed only recently, because they were still fresh.

"Oh, jeez. I was afraid of this," Gannon said.

"Afraid of what?" I asked.

"That's a fairy circle!"

"Okay, I'll humor you," I said, slightly annoyed. "What's a fairy circle?"

"They mark a spot where elves and fairies have danced. If you step inside the circle, something bad will happen."

"Like what?" I asked, rolling my eyes.

"They say the fairies will take control of you. And the fairies that set these traps, they aren't the good kind of fairies. They're the wicked kind."

"The things you fall for baffle me."

"Let's get going. The sooner we find our way out of this forest, the better."

Gannon is letting his imagination get the best of him. At the moment, he actually thinks we're being followed by elves. I am trying to ignore him and do my best to get our bearings in this forest. So far, no luck, but I'm still confident we are headed in the right direction and will find our way back to the O'Leary's soon.

GANNON

Right, so we've gone from being just a "wee bit" lost to being totally and completely lost, and I'm starting to freak out a little!

Okay, a lot.

My opinion is that we're farther away from Shamrock Farm than we've ever been, and judging by the mossy growth blanketing everything and the little rocks bubbling up like mushrooms (that might actually be fairy houses) and the creepy mist floating through the trees and the even spookier hoots of owls that I keep hearing—yeah, I'd say we're dead smack in the middle of the spookiest part of the forest.

Here's the thing: I don't like being lost in spooky forests.

It makes me paranoid. Let me give an example. Earlier, I had this weird, shivers-down-my-spine suspicion that we were being watched, when out of the corner of my eye, I saw something moving in the bushes. That's when I was sure of it.

We *were* being watched!

I kept my eyes locked on those bushes, and that's when I saw it. Almost completely camouflaged among the brush was another living creature. A big and stoic creature with a huge set of antlers and dark, oval-shaped eyes.

The creature? It was an Irish red deer!

Boy, was I relieved.

"Wyatt," I whispered, pointing. "Check it out."

"Wow," Wyatt said, "that's one big stag."

An Irish red deer

The red deer stood perfectly still, like one of the huge bronze animal sculptures my dad's made, with a stare so intense, I felt like I needed to acknowledge him or something. Finally, I held up my hand, almost like I was waving "hi." As soon as I did, the deer sprung sideways like it had hopped off a trampoline. Two hops and I'd already lost him in the forest.

Okay, the fact that it was only a deer was definitely a relief, as I said before, but who knows what we'll run into next—a leprechaun, a banshee, a knife-wielding psycho? Worst part is, nightfall's creeping in on us. All I can say is this, if we don't find our way out of the forest soon, I might go completely loony!

WYATT

OCTOBER 8, 11:08 PM
LOCATION UNKNOWN
46° FAHRENHEIT, 8° CELSIUS
WIND 10-15 MPH, DRIZZLE

It was late. Dark. Cold. Clouds moved over the moon. Rain came. Heavy, then heavier.

We were both shivering and realized we'd become hypothermic if we didn't find a dry place to take shelter and start a fire. For what must have been a half hour, we sloshed through the muck until we finally came upon a gigantic fallen tree that was hollowed out at the base and just big enough to take cover inside. My whacko brother had me check to make sure it wasn't the house of an elf before he agreed to climb inside the trunk. Once I'd proven to him that the space was empty, we settled in and were able to start a small fire with the flint rocks I have in my backpack and a bed of dry moss.

I'm anticipating that the sky will be a solid sheet of gray tomorrow, so the sun will be of no help in determining our direction. However, we just came across a river and I'm hoping it's the same one that runs through Shamrock Farm. Knowing that the farm sits downriver from the forest, we will hike in the direction of the current as soon as the sun comes up.

Time to wrap up this journal entry and get some sleep. Spent the day scrambling through the dense woods and may end up doing the same tomorrow if we can't find our way back to the O'Leary's. Point in fact, we have no food, very few supplies, and not the foggiest idea where we are.

GANNON

OCTOBER 9, EARLY MORNING
MY HEAD STILL GROGGY, THE FOREST STILL FOGGY

Oh man, I had the craziest dream last night!

Then again, maybe it wasn't a dream at all. Maybe it was real! In this forest, it's sometimes hard to tell the difference.

Anyhow, I've got to record what I remember of it before we head out for the day and I forget all the details. So, in the dream or whatever it was, I was just sitting there when all of a sudden here comes this little bulb of light floating through the forest. It kept coming my way, growing larger, its rainbow aura casting a colorful glow in the trees. Finally, it was close enough for me to make out what it was. The bulb of light—it was a fairy!

The fairy was tiny, about the size of a dragonfly, and hovered right in front of me, a foot or so above the ground. She had long blonde hair and the beautiful facial features of a princess and was wearing this flowing white dress. The pulsating prism of light that surrounded her put off this weird positive energy. I mean, I wasn't scared at all. Actually, I felt calm, like I knew this fairy wanted to help.

"The gift is the key," the fairy said softly.

"The gift?" I asked.

"Yes, the gift. It is the key."

"What does that mean?"

A sad look came over her face. The glow that surrounded her began to fade. She was disappearing right before my eyes.

"Wait!" I said. "Don't go. What gift? I don't understand. Please tell me what we're supposed to do."

Just before she vanished, she spoke again. Her voice was frail and haunting.

"If you don't stop Moloney, then who? All of Ireland is depending on you."

With the final whisper, she faded into the wind.

I sat up like a shot, wide awake and out of breath. The

fairy's voice echoed in my head. Quietly, I repeated what she had said.

"The gift is the key. If you don't stop Moloney, then who? All of Ireland is depending on you."

Wyatt was writing in his journal and looked up at me.

"What did you say?" he asked.

"Nothing," I said, not wanting to give him the opportunity to dismiss this mysterious experience as an absurd product of my imagination.

A chill danced its way down my spine. My heart was thumping loudly in my chest and I had goosebumps all over my body. I'm telling you, there is something seriously freaky about this forest.

As my brain worked to shake away the grogginess of a poor night's sleep, I struggled to make a distinction between the dream world and reality. I wondered, was I losing my mind or had this whole thing actually happened? Maybe Wyatt was right about me reading too many Irish fairy tales. Whether it was real or not, I think there's something to it. After all, dreams aren't for nothing. They have meaning. I've always believed that. So, even if this was a dream, I can't discount the important message the fairy had for us. Now, if I could just figure out what in the world she meant . . .

WYATT

Land of the Leprechaun

We were hiking this morning at a good pace, when Gannon stopped abruptly. Slowly, he raised his arm and pointed into the forest. His eyes were as wide as golf balls.

"I think I just saw something floating up in the trees," he whispered.

"Would you stop already?" I said. "Your paranoia is really starting to annoy me."

"No, I'm serious this time!"

I looked around.

"I don't see anything," I said.

"It's way out there."

"I think you're hallucinating."

"Jeez, Wyatt. I bet it's a banshee."

"Stop."

"It's a banshee coming to deliver a message of doom. That's what they do, you know? They show up just before you die. Oh man, we're goners."

"I refuse to listen to your fairy-tale babble."

"There, I just saw it again," Gannon said, pointing. "I'm serious. There is something out there."

"It's probably another red deer."

"No, I told you. It's moving around up in the trees, which means it has to be some kind of mythical creature. Seriously, what else moves through the air like that?"

Just then, a swooshing sound swept right over our heads. Gannon screamed and hit the dirt, covering his head with his hands. I turned around to see what had just swooped overhead. Behind us, perched on a branch, was a beautiful falcon. It was the falcon that Grace had trained. It was Oscar!

Gannon was lying in the mud, head covered, a total blubbering mess.

"Please don't tell us that we're going to die," he was saying. "Please don't tell us that we're going to die."

"Gannon, I just thought of something else that moves through the air."

"What?"

"A bird."

"A bird?"

"Get up. It's Oscar. He came to pay us a visit."

Gannon lifted his head from the muck and looked at the great falcon.

"Oscar!" he shouted. "Oh my gosh, are you a sight for delirious eyes."

"Check it out. He has something with him."

Behind Oscar's head was a tightly rolled piece of paper secured by a leather strap. I approached Oscar and slowly extended my arm, careful not to scare him. Oscar blinked and turned his head, but remained perched on the branch. Once I slid the paper free, Oscar immediately took flight, heading back in the direction from which he came.

I unrolled the paper.

"What is it?" Gannon asked.

"It's a note from Grace. And a map."

"Hold on, let me get this straight," Gannon said. "Oscar just found us in the middle of this forest and delivered a message from Grace?"

"Appears so."

"Oh man, that is so cool! So, what's the note say?"

I read it aloud:

Gannon & Wyatt:

I hope this note finds you safe. Moloney's goons came looking for you, but Da sent them away in a fury. Since you've been out two nights, I imagine you must be lost and hungry. I drew a detailed map of the forest so you can find your way back to the farm, and made a list of edible plants that will help sustain you in the meantime. Be careful to stay out of sight. If Moloney's men catch you, Da says there's no telling what they'll do.

Your friend,
Grace

"Okay, first order of business," Gannon said. "Food! So, what's safe to eat in this forest?"

I looked at the list Grace had made, which also had drawings next to each plant so they would be easier to identify. When you have to resort to eating plants in the forest, it's critical to know what is safe and what is not. There are plants that can make you very sick. Some are even deadly.

"Clovers are edible," I said. "So are dandelions. And she said we may come across wild asparagus."

"I know I've seen some clovers around," Gannon said. "And dandelions are those little yellow flowers, right?"

"Right."

"Let's start our trek back to the farmhouse. We'll keep our eyes peeled for food along the way."

"Okay, let me take a look at the map . . ."

Gannon ripped it out of my hand before I had a chance.

"No offense, bro," he said. "I mean, you're a smart guy and all, but your map-reading skills are a little less than stellar. What do you say I take the lead on this one?"

Gannon is no expert cartographer either, but I was too tired to argue.

"Be my guest," I said.

It's been a little over an hour and according to the map it looks like we're about halfway to the farm. Getting the note from Grace gave us a second wind, but no amount of enthusiasm can stand up to our hunger. We're shaky, cold, and our stomachs ache. Just so happens, we're in a very muddy, water-logged area of the forest and haven't seen any of the edible plants. If we don't find something to eat soon, I don't know if we'll have enough energy to make it back to the farm.

GANNON

A patch of clovers . . . or lunch

Grace is a guardian angel! Oscar too!

By the time we came across something to eat, my legs were like boiled spaghetti and I was hardly able to hold my head up straight. No joke, I thought I was about to keel over—caput, done, dead as a doornail—when all of a sudden I spotted a grassy slope that was exposed to the sunlight and covered in yellow flowers.

Our food!

Right away, I dropped to my knees and tore up a handful of fully bloomed dandelions. There were large patches of clovers, too. No wild asparagus, but that's okay. Never been a huge asparagus fan anyhow.

"Can you just eat these flowers whole?" I asked.

"Sure can," Wyatt said. "Give it a try."

I took a little nibble of the stem first. It was leafy tasting, pretty much like a bland garden salad. Not half bad, though. Next, I popped a flower into my mouth. I expected it to pop with sweetness, but it was actually a little bitter and had the consistency of damp wax paper or something. The clovers tasted pretty similar to the leaves of the dandelions.

A curious red-coated fox joined our feast, sniffing around our backpacks while Wyatt and I sat in the soft, soggy moss and proceeded to polish off as much vegetation as we could stand.

"You won't find any food in there," I said and held out some greens to the fox. "But you're welcome to some yummy clovers."

The fox sniffed my hand but refused the offer. Still, he stuck around, lying in the grass as we filled our backpacks with an extra helping of greenery, just in case. I have to say, before this snack I was so hungry I'd have traded my brother for a hot basket of fish and chips—still might, actually—but we definitely ate enough to relieve the hunger pangs and keep us going for a while.

As we finished up, sporadic gusts of wind came roaring up the slope into the trees, shaking the branches and making the forest seem almost anxious, as if it was trying to warn us of something. The fox noticed it too. He sat up and his ears rotated forward.

A wide-eyed Irish fox

Between the gusts of wind there was a sound that seemed out of place in the forest. I wanted to ignore it, to pretend it was nothing, but it was growing more noticeable by the minute.

All of a sudden, the fox sprang to his feet.

I looked at Wyatt.

"They're coming for us," he said.

The sound, it was dogs.

Bloodhounds!

The barking grew louder. Somehow these dogs had picked up our scent. Like a flash, the fox darted down the hill and disappeared into the forest. We jumped up and followed the fox's path, even though it wasn't very well suited for two-legged creatures like us. The slope was wet and muddy and we went slipping and sliding all the way down to the river. To prevent the dogs from keeping our scent, we took to the water, running upriver for a stretch. Then we scrambled up a gulch carved out by a stream that Grace had marked on the map. At the top of the gulch, the land leveled out some, and we continued running in shallow water along the banks for a good 15-20 minutes.

Desperate for rest, we've taken shelter under some rocks. As I write, our breath fills the air with clouds of steam. Outside, the rain is coming down in sheets, which I think helped us shake the dogs by washing away our scent and any footprints we may have left behind. Still, I'm wrecked with nerves at the thought of being caught by these nutcases. I can't even imagine what our parents would do if they knew the mess we'd gotten ourselves into.

Good news is that we're not far from the farm. Looking at Grace's map, I'd guess it's about 30 to 45 minutes away, tops. Our plan is to meet with Grace and decide what to do with the evidence we collected.

Then, I don't know, I guess we'll have to go back into hiding until Moloney's men stop looking for us. Or maybe Mr. O'Leary will let us stay in the barn until things blow over. Lots to figure out, but getting the evidence in the right hands is the first and most important step in bringing Moloney to justice.

WYATT
OCTOBER 9, 4:03 PM

When we finally caught sight of the O'Learys' farmhouse through the trees, Gannon and I could not have been happier.

"Oh, what a beautiful sight!" Gannon said, smacking me on the back. "We made it!"

Unfortunately, our celebration was short lived. As we came through the woods at the far end of the property, all we could hear was shouting.

"Sounds like something serious is going on," Gannon whispered.

Keeping just inside the edge of the forest, we moved closer.

"Over my dead body!" I heard someone yell.

Peeking through the brush, we could see that Mr. O'Leary was in a heated argument with two men in dark suits. One man I recognized as Moloney's bodyguard.

Mr. O'Leary was livid, waving his arms in the air and

shouting like a man possessed. Grace stood quietly on the porch.

"What do you think is going on?" I asked.

"Who knows," Gannon said. "But whatever it is, Mr. O isn't too happy about it. Let's see if we can move closer and listen in."

Gannon and I crept quietly along the edge of the forest until we were close enough to hear the conversation. The bodyguard removed a letter from his inside jacket pocket and handed it to Mr. O'Leary, who immediately tore it to shreds and threw the pieces in the man's face.

"I'll say it again!" Mr. O'Leary shouted. "Over my dead body!"

"That can be arranged," Moloney's bodyguard said.

Mr. O'Leary and the bodyguard stood toe to toe. It looked like one of them was about to throw a punch. Mr. O'Leary's a tough chap, but he'd be no match for that huge beast. And after the way Moloney's bodyguard had threatened us, I was afraid something terrible was about to happen to Grace's father.

"Get off my property before I call the Garda!" Mr. O'Leary shouted. "I can't stand the sight of you for another second!"

The other man calmly grabbed the bodyguard by the arm and led him to the car.

"You haven't seen the last of us!" the bodyguard shouted before tearing out of the driveway.

Mr. O'Leary screamed some words I'd rather not record in my journal, said something to Grace, and then stormed into the house.

Grace sat down on the steps of the porch and put her face in her hands. Since Moloney's men had gone, we felt it was safe to come out of hiding. Gannon and I ran to Grace to see what we could do. She heard us coming and looked up.

"Gannon and Wyatt," she said, tears in her eyes. "Oh, thank goodness you're here. I need your help."

"What's going on, Grace?" Gannon asked.

"Moloney's men made an offer to buy our farm," Grace said, choking back tears. "Apparently, they need our land to expand his farm complex. Da wouldn't sell for any price, but the offer they made was so low it was insulting. They said Moloney was going to put us out of business one way or another, so we'd be smart to take their offer while we had the chance."

"I told you," Gannon said, "Kilgore Moloney is just plain evil."

"Da said that it's all gone too far. Said it's time he did something about it. Then he told me he's leaving and won't be back for a while."

"What do you think he's going to do?"

"I don't know, but I'm afraid he'll do something rash. And if he does, he could get himself into trouble or even hurt. I honestly don't think he's in his right mind."

"I've got an idea," Gannon said. "When he leaves, do you think he'll take the pickup truck?"

"I'm sure he will, why?"

"Wyatt and I will go with him," he said.

"He would never allow it," Grace said.

"Don't worry, he won't know. Follow me!"

Gannon took off like a shot and we followed him around the side of the house to Mr. O'Leary's truck.

"Give me your backpack," Gannon said, ripping it from my back. He handed our packs to Grace.

"Stash these in our room for now," Gannon said. "Good news is that we got all sorts of great evidence against Moloney. When we get back we'll figure out where we should take it."

Mr. O'Leary yelled for Grace.

"Quick, Wyatt," Gannon said, climbing into the bed of the truck. "Get in and Grace will cover us with the tarp."

"Are you joking?" I asked. "That's a terrible idea."

"Well, if you have a better one, I'm all ears."

I needed to think, but there was no time.

"Just get in the truck before Mr. O'Leary comes out and sees us," Gannon said. "That way we can help keep him out of trouble."

"Oh please, Wyatt," Grace said. "I'm begging you. I can't risk losing my da. He is everything to me. Please help."

"Come on, Wyatt. Do it for Grace."

"Okay, I'll do it," I said and climbed in next to Gannon. "Cover us up, Grace. We'll do our best to keep your father in line, but you know it won't be easy."

"Grace!" Mr. O'Leary shouted. "Where are the keys to the truck?"

"Coming, Da!" Grace yelled as she threw the tarp over the top of us. "Stay still so he doesn't see you. And please, do whatever it takes to keep him from doing something foolish."

"Grace!" Mr. O'Leary shouted again.

"I'll be right there, Da!"

Not more than a minute later, Mr. O'Leary climbed into his truck and took off like a Formula One racecar driver. It's a miracle Gannon and I even survived the ride. Our skulls kept crashing into one another as Mr. O'Leary gunned it around the twists and turns of the potholed road that led all the way to the Moloney Factory Farm Complex. When he blew through a metal gate at the far end of the property, its mangled remains crashed over the rooftop and nearly took our heads off. That's when I made a mental note never to ride in the back of a pickup truck again.

The terror I felt on that wild ride faded minutes later when we witnessed an incident I would have never believed if I hadn't seen it with my own eyes.

Mr. O'Leary was in such a fit of rage he didn't even turn off the truck engine, just put it in park and jumped out. Before we knew what was happening, he had disappeared into the nearest warehouse. The same one Gannon and I snuck into a couple days ago.

"What do you think he's up to?" I asked.

"If I know Mr. O'Leary, he's about to give someone a piece of his mind."

We heard the sound of a metal crank being wound, and one of the large garage doors started to open.

"Should we go down there?" Gannon asked. "We promised Grace we'd keep him out of trouble."

"We probably should."

But before we even made two steps, we were stopped in our tracks by a totally unexpected sight—pigs by the dozens, then hundreds, pouring out of the warehouse. Mr. O'Leary was setting them free!

"Go! Go! Go!" Mr. O'Leary shouted as he smacked one pig after another on the hindquarter. "You're caged no more! Run free! Run, my friends! Run!"

"Oh my gosh," Gannon said. "This might just be the best thing I've ever seen."

"But I have a feeling it's not going to end well," I said.

"We should help him."

"You want to get arrested too?"

"This is totally justified. Those animals deserve to be set free."

"I agree, but this is a violation of private property and Moloney's going to make him pay for it. I guarantee you that."

"I don't care. What's right is right. And this is right! Today we liberate the animals!"

I tried to grab Gannon, but he shook free and took off

running for the warehouse. I managed to catch him from behind and had to tackle him to the ground to keep him from going any farther.

"Get off me, Wyatt! I'm going to help Mr. O save the animals and that's all there is to it!"

"I can't let you do that!"

A siren rang out. Red lights were flashing inside the warehouse. Men in protective yellow suits were running every which way. There had to be five hundred pigs now, maybe more, all free of the warehouse and scampering up the hillside. Several men were trying to round them up. Others were trying to keep the rest of the pigs from escaping the warehouse. It was total chaos.

I saw Mr. O'Leary slip out a side door and run to the adjacent warehouse where he again disappeared inside. "I'm going to let you up," I said to Gannon. "But you have to promise me you won't do anything stupid!"

"I'm not promising anything! Just get off me!"

I had no choice but to let Gannon up. We needed to stop Mr. O'Leary. The more damage he did, the worse it was going to be for him in the end.

Gannon and I ran around the side of the warehouse just in time to see the large garage door open. I could hear gates clanking and the collective moos of frantic cows. Before we could get to the door, a stampeding herd came charging out of the warehouse.

"This is crazy!" Gannon shouted. "But I love it! Go, Mr. O! Set the animals free!"

"We better get out of the way," I said and took off as hundreds of cattle came thundering up the hill.

Mr. O'Leary was running with them in the middle of the herd, hardly visible over the high backs of the black and white spotted cows. Two of Moloney's men were chasing after him. When Mr. O'Leary noticed the men in pursuit, he weaved his way out of the herd and sprinted up the hill toward his truck.

"He doesn't even know we're here!" Gannon shouted. "We have to catch him or he'll leave us!"

Mr. O'Leary made it to the truck in a hurry, jumped in the driver's seat, and tore away, his tires spitting mud behind him as the truck slid sideways. We were about to be left behind.

"Wait!" Gannon shouted as we ran to catch up.

Mr. O'Leary's attempt to flee in such a hurry had the truck sliding all over the place, and as it came around sideways, he spotted us making our way up the hill.

"Wait for us!" Gannon shouted.

Mr. O'Leary slammed on the brakes and stuck his head out the window.

"Gannon and Wyatt?" he said, looking very surprised to see us.

"We'll explain later!" I yelled.

"Hurry up and jump in the back!" he shouted.

We did as he said and he gunned it for the gate that he'd already plowed over. As we drove through the opening, two of Moloney's trucks came speeding up the hill in hot pursuit. Mr. O'Leary slid open the small window to the pickup bed and yelled to us:

"Hold on tight! We're taking a little shortcut I know!"

He jerked the wheel to the right and we sped off into the forest. The truck was getting knocked all over the place, thumping over rocks and fallen trees. Gannon and I were bouncing around in the back like rodeo cowboys. I thought for sure the tires were about to blow out or that we'd crash into a tree, but the path through the forest actually leveled off, making the drive more smooth. Mr. O'Leary slowed the truck and looked back toward the road. The two trucks that were chasing us went racing by, unaware we'd taken a detour into the trees.

"We lost them," Mr. O'Leary said and turned to speak to us through the small window. "Now I can deal with the two of you. First of all, what in God's name are you doing here?"

"We promised Grace we wouldn't let you do anything crazy," Gannon said, "so we hid in the back of the truck."

"Looks like we failed on our promise though," I added.

"Agh, this is none of your business anyway," Mr. O'Leary said. "You shouldn't have gotten yourselves mixed up in it in the first place. You went snooping around the complex when I told you not to. You're quite lucky you weren't caught. You might have gone missing. Permanently! Where are your heads?"

"With all due respect, sir," Gannon said, "what we just witnessed, which was completely justified and totally awesome in my opinion, was also a thousand times crazier than anything Wyatt and I did. We were just trying to gather evidence that might help get Moloney's place shut down. You basically led an animal revolt!"

"It's true, Mr. O'Leary," I added. "You did go on a bit of a rampage back there."

Mr. O'Leary took off his driver's cap and wiped sweat off his forehead with a handkerchief.

"I honestly don't know what got into me, lads," he said. "I was fed up. The anger and desperation I felt, it just boiled over and something in me snapped."

Mr. O'Leary put his cap back on.

"Why don't you two get in the front of the truck," he said, suddenly solemn. "I need to get back to Gracie and tell her what I've done."

Gannon and I sat in the front of the truck the rest of the drive to Shamrock Farm. Not a word was spoken. Mr. O'Leary obviously knew there were going to be consequences for his actions. Conscquences that would likely be severe. As we drove in silence, the torment on his face led me to believe that he was thinking about what might happen to the one thing he loved most in this world. The one thing he loved even more than the farm. He was thinking about his daughter, Grace.

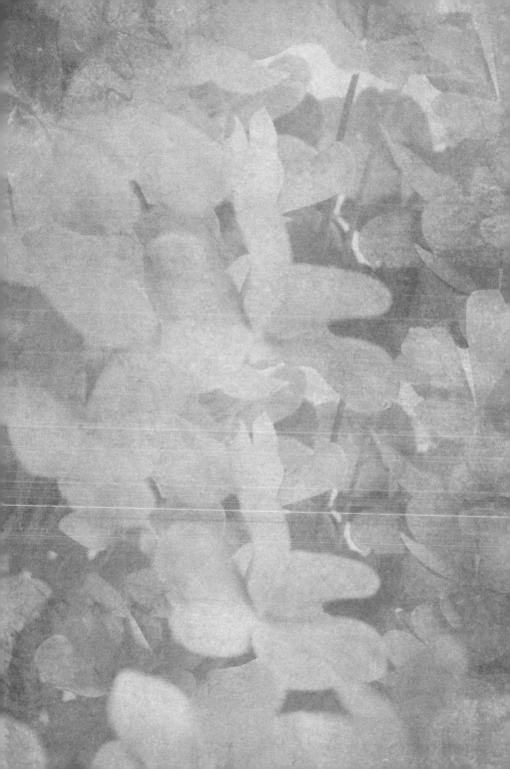

PART III

THE LUCK OF THE IRISH

GANNON
OCTOBER 9
SHAMROCK FARM

The pickup truck came to a screeching halt at the front of the house. Grace came out the front door.

"I've been worried sick," she said. "Is everything okay?"

"They're coming for me, Gracie," Mr. O'Leary said, running from his truck.

"Who's coming for you?"

Mr. O'Leary stepped onto the porch and put his hands on his daughter's shoulders.

"Moloney's men," he said. "Maybe the Garda, too. I'm sorry. I lost my head today, sweetheart. Busted into Moloney's complex and set some of his animals loose."

"By *some* he means hundreds," Gannon said.

"Then we should leave now," Grace said, panicked. "Let's

get out of here, Da. We can go somewhere until everything settles down."

"I never wanted to harm anyone," Mr. O'Leary continued. "You know I'm no criminal. Never broke the law in my life. God's honest truth. But Moloney was hurting us, hurting so many other farmers, and I was desperate to stop him."

"Please, Da. Let's go. I don't want them to take you away from me."

Grace was desperate and started to cry. Mr. O'Leary took her in his arms.

"I'm so sorry I've done this to you, Gracie. I went and made a real mess of things. Your ma would have my neck, she would. I pray that you will one day forgive me."

All at once an entire caravan of cars came speeding down the O'Leary's driveway. There were five cars total; the two cars in the front had flashing blue lights and the word "Garda" painted on the side. At the sight, Grace fell to her knees sobbing. Mr. O'Leary knelt down beside her and cradled her head into his chest.

"You boys make yourselves scarce," Mr. O'Leary said. "Moloney's men will still be looking for you. But this is all my doing and I need to handle it alone. There's no need for you to be mixed up any further! Go now before you're seen!"

We obeyed Mr. O'Leary orders, taking off for the small garden on the side of the house and hiding in a section of high cornstalks.

"Stay down and don't move," Wyatt said.

The caravan came to a stop in front of the farmhouse. Moloney's bodyguard stepped out of one of the cars. So did Kilgore Moloney and a couple of men wearing yellow suits from the complex. One of them immediately identified Mr. O'Leary.

"That is the man!" Mr. Moloney yelled. "Cormac O'Leary! I have eyewitnesses! He is the man who raided my farm and wreaked havoc on my operation! I demand he be punished to the full extent of the law!"

Two Garda officers approached the porch.

"Mr. Cormac O'Leary," one of them said.

"Yes," he said somberly.

"You are under arrest for destruction of private property."

"I didn't destroy anything," Mr. O'Leary said. "I just let some animals out of those awful cages."

"We suggest you make this easy on yourself and come with us."

Grace broke down.

"Please don't take my da!" she pleaded. "I am begging you!"

"Is there another adult who can stay with your daughter?" one of the Garda asked. "Her ma, perhaps?"

"I'm afraid not," Mr. O'Leary said. "Her ma passed some time ago."

The Garda officers looked at one another.

"I am sorry, sir," one of them said. "If there is no other legal guardian, your daughter will have to come with us as well."

The scene that unfolded next was almost too difficult to bear. Mr. O'Leary was put in handcuffs. As he was escorted toward the car, he insisted that what he had done was justified, that it was done for the good of the animals, the good of the people of Ireland. Mr. O'Leary shouted that Moloney's pollution was destroying the land and that his treatment of the animals was utterly shameful.

"Moloney is the criminal here!" Mr. O'Leary went on. "Why does no one have the courage to acknowledge this? You should be taking him to jail!"

Mr. Moloney didn't even bother to respond.

Grace was clinging to her father, her arms wrapped tightly around his chest. It took the strength of several men to pull her away. She fought and screamed like her life was coming to a tragic end. In a way, I suppose it was.

During all the commotion, Grace's faithful falcon, Oscar, did his best to intervene, dive-bombing the men who carried Grace to the van. He would swoop in low with his razor sharp talons extended, causing the men to duck and even dive into the dirt once or twice. When one of the Garda removed a pistol from his holster and took aim at the bird, Grace shouted, "Oscar, forest!" At her command, the bird extended his wings and banked left, safely camouflaging itself in the trees before the Garda could fire a shot.

"Mr. O'Leary must pay for his crime," Kilgore Moloney said ruthlessly. "If he remains in prison for years to come, so be it."

"What's going to happen to my daughter?" Mr. O'Leary yelled as he was being led away.

"She'll be transported to a facility in Dublin," one of the men said.

"What facility?" he asked.

"That is none of your concern at the moment."

"I demand that you tell me!" Mr. O'Leary shouted as he was forced inside the van. "That is my daughter! Please tell me where she's going! I beg you to . . ."

At that, the door of the van was slammed, drowning out his desperate cries.

"We should do something," I whispered.

"Just stay put," Wyatt said. "If we show ourselves, we'll be taken away too. Probably locked up. Then we won't be able to help at all."

Once the last of the cars had disappeared around the bend, Wyatt and I crawled out of hiding. I think we were both in shock because we just stood there, tears in our eyes, quietly gazing over the fields of ailing crops. The green hillside to the east was spotted with dozens of sheep nibbling in the grass, all of them oblivious to the catastrophe that had just unfolded on the farm.

My head sank. Everything was a mess. I wanted to help in some way, but I didn't have a clue what to do. It had been made clear we were fighting forces much more powerful than ourselves. For a minute, I honestly felt like giving up.

Then, as I wiped tears from my eyes, I noticed a small

patch of clovers among the grass. I knelt down to take a closer look and couldn't believe what I saw.

"Check it out, Wyatt," I said with a sudden rush of enthusiasm. "You know what this is?"

Wyatt knelt beside me.

"It's a species of herbaceous plant."

I shook my head.

"Sometimes your nerdiness blinds you to the magic that's right in front of your eyes."

"What are you talking about?"

"It's a four-leaf clover! They're so rare, and finding one brings good luck! This is exactly what we need to help us turn this whole situation around!"

"Oh, come on," Wyatt said and rolled his eyes. "Didn't you learn your lesson with the Blarney Stone? All these Irish tales, they're just stories made up by people with really good imaginations."

"Whatever, Wyatt," I said, dismissing my brother. "Four-leaf clovers are good luck. If you don't want to believe it, that's your problem."

The lucky four-leaf clover

I gently plucked the clover and held it in the palm of my hand. I'm not joking, the energy coming off that little thing made my arm tingle. Gently, I placed the clover in my chest pocket. A sudden confidence came over me.

I looked my brother straight in the eyes.

"New plan, Wyatt," I said. "We're going to Dublin!"

"Wait, why?"

"To meet with government officials and prove to all of them that Kilgore Moloney is a criminal!"

"How do you know Moloney isn't paying off officials in Dublin too?"

"He couldn't be paying off everyone, could he? We'll bring

the samples, photos, and video and make sure everyone in Ireland's government knows what he's up to. The EPA, Parliament, the prime minister, everyone! If we make our voices heard, we're bound to find someone who will take a stand!"

"Sounds good in theory," Wyatt said, "but how do you plan to pull it off? These things take time. There are protocols to follow. First we have to build our case. Turn over our samples to the EPA's labs and wait for them to verify my results. Photos and video need to be circulated. Reports have to be written. All evidence then has to be submitted to government officials. Then, based on the evidence, a course of action will be mapped out."

"Oh, come on. We'll be old men before that all happens. We need to figure out how to bypass the protocols and make the government take action now!"

"Gannon, we can't just waltz into the Irish Parliament, step up to the podium, and say, 'Uh, excuse me everyone. If you could lend me your ear for just a moment, I'd like to inform you of some illegal polluting that's happening in County Kerry.'"

A smile came over my face.

"Actually, that's a great idea, Wyatt."

"Please tell me you're joking."

Out of the blue, I remembered the fairy that had passed on the cryptic message when we were lost in the forest.

"It's just like the fairy told me," I said to myself. "The gift is the key."

"Excuse me?" Wyatt said. "Did you say *fairy?*"

"Now I know what she meant! The gift, Wyatt! The gift of gab! It's the key!"

"Okay, it's official. You've completely lost your mind."

"Quick, let's grab our backpacks and some food from the house. We have to get to the bus station pronto. The sooner we're in Dublin the better. That's where they're taking Grace and that's where we can find the people who can actually do something about Moloney!"

WYATT

OCTOBER 9, 9:48 PM
EN ROUTE TO DUBLIN
55° FAHRENHEIT, 13° CELSIUS

Making our way into town, we cut through the forest to keep out of sight and avoid Moloney's men. Eventually, we found our way to the station and hid in the alley until we were allowed to board the bus to Dublin. We were suspicious of everyone who passed and kept looking over our shoulders to see if any of Moloney's men were coming for us. It doesn't seem that we are being followed, but we can't be sure.

Right now we are about an hour into the three-and-a-half hour bus trip, so we've had time to think things over. The plan is as follows: First, we're going to find my mom at the orphanage. Her contacts there should be able to help us determine where they're holding Grace. Maybe we can even get her out. Second, while Gannon and my mom are tracking down Grace, I am going to find a photo developer and print several copies of our photographs from Moloney's Factory Farm Complex. Third, we're all going to meet at Leinster House on Kildare Street, where we will distribute all of the photographs and video, along with the air and water samples to members of Parliament and Ireland's Environmental Protection Agency. Just seeing the gruesome living conditions of the animals should be enough to get them to launch an investigation. And once they have official test results showing the water and air pollution being caused by the operation, Mr. Moloney will be forced to pay for what he's done. All of this evidence might even help get Mr. O'Leary pardoned.

What I'm worried about most is that this whole process could take weeks, even months. Given the power and influence Mr. Moloney has in this country, even if we do get an investigation started, it's possible he could get the whole thing shut down. Dealing with someone as corrupt as Moloney, it is impossible to predict what might happen.

GANNON
OCTOBER 10
DUBLIN, IRELAND

Last night we rolled into Dublin really late.

Stepping off the bus, we ran a few blocks to make sure no one was following us and then set out for the orphanage.

By the time we got there it was locked up and we couldn't reach my mom and didn't have enough money for a hotel, so we wound up wandering the streets for what seemed like hours looking for a safe place to sleep. The boulevards and squares of Dublin that are crowded with pedestrians by day were nearly deserted. As for those who were still out wandering, let's just say they weren't the type you'd want to pal around with.

Streetlights bathed us in an orange glow as we passed underneath. The moon was out too, nearly full and very bright. Around every corner slender shadows were on the march, stretching across the brick walkways and up the walls of old buildings.

We thought we might be able to find a place to sleep on the grounds of Trinity College, but the spiky metal gates surrounding campus were locked and climbing over the top might have resulted in an unintended piercing, so we kept on. Not long after, we found ourselves in Merrion Square Park, somewhere near the city center. Following the pedestrian path through a canopy of trees whose leaves shook in the wind, we came across a large rock with a statue of the Irish writer Oscar Wilde sitting on top.

"Check it out," I said. "We could totally sleep behind this rock. No one will see us back there."

Statue of famed Irish writer, Oscar Wilde

"At this point, I'll sleep anywhere," Wyatt said.

As we were settling in, a man popped his head out of the shrubs.

"This spot is taken," he said in a gruff voice.

Wyatt and I nearly jumped out of our boots.

"Did you not see my bed, lads?" he asked.

A few feet away, spread out on the ground, was a sheet of cardboard. A plastic grocery bag stuffed with trash appeared to serve as his pillow. The disheveled man stepped out of the bushes. His clothes were in tatters. I noticed he was carrying a stack of newspapers.

"We're sorry, sir," I said, not wanting any trouble. "We'll move on."

"Here, take some of these with you," he said, handing us each a set of newspapers. "It's a bit nippy tonight."

"Ah, *The Irish Times*," I said, taking the newspaper in my hands.

"It's a good read but a better blanket."

"We're very appreciative," Wyatt said. "Have a good night."

"You too, lads."

The man tipped his frayed cap, and we continued on our way.

Blankets in hand, we roamed aimlessly for another stretch before finally deciding to take our chances and bunk on a set of uncomfortable wooden benches tucked away in the far end of a hotel courtyard. Right next to the benches was a bronze statue of the famous Irish author James Joyce, wearing a fedora and sporting a cane.

Another famous Irish writer, James Joyce

"Funny how we keep running into Ireland's literary icons tonight," Wyatt said.

"It's a sign, Wyatt."

"Yeah, it's a sign we're homeless."

"Mr. Joyce, if you don't mind," I said, snuggling up on the bench, "please keep an eye on us until morning. Thank you kindly, sir."

Wrapped like a sausage in the sports section of *The Irish Times*, I was awoken some hours later by a man wearing a long-tailed gray suit and a top hat. It was one of the hotel's bellmen.

"Are you a guest of the hotel?" the bellman asked.

"If I was, do you think I'd be sleeping on this bench?" I replied.

"Then you have to leave. And I suggest you do so before the manager calls the Garda."

"Thanks for the warning."

I stood up and gave Wyatt a kick to wake him.

"I'm up," he said, popping up from the bench.

"Grab your stuff," I said. "We've overstayed our welcome here."

The dark blue sky was growing lighter with the first rays of the morning sun. We grabbed our backpacks and gathered up all the newspaper.

"Thanks for the accommodations," I said. "Oh, one last thing." I held out the newspaper. "Do you recycle?"

"We do," he said. "Green bin on your way out. Now, bugger off."

Pulling our jackets tight around us to fend off the morning chill, we hit the sidewalk. It was time to put our plan into action. Wyatt caught a bus to Grafton Street to get prints made of all the pictures, while I hopped a bus that dropped me a few blocks from the orphanage where my mom was volunteering.

Oh man, was it hilarious to see my mom's face when I came strolling in the door. I mean, her jaw just about hit the floor. You'd have thought a leprechaun had just walked in or something.

"Hey there, Mom," I said.

"Gannon," she said. "What in the world are you doing here? I thought you had a few weeks left on the farm?"

"Change of plans."

"What's going on?"

"Wyatt and I have some official business here in Dublin. And we need your help."

"Where is Wyatt? Is everything okay?"

"I don't really have time to explain everything at the moment. We need to meet Wyatt at Leinster House in less than an hour."

"Leinster House?"

"It's where the Irish Parliament meets."

"What are you talking about, Gannon?"

"First things first, Mom. Can you help me track down a friend? It's the daughter of the farmer we were working for. Just yesterday she was brought to a facility here in Dublin. We're assuming an orphanage. I don't know which one, but her name is Grace O'Leary."

"Grace O'Leary," my mom said. "The name actually sounds familiar."

My mom sat down, opened a book, and began scanning the names.

"That's what I thought. Grace O'Leary arrived last night."

"Here?" I asked. "At this orphanage? Come on, Mom. Don't mess with me."

"I'm not messing with you, Gannon. Her name is right here on the register."

"I knew the luck of the Irish was bound to strike sooner or later! Okay, Mom, listen. Grace's farm has been in her family for six generations, but it's under threat and we're trying to help save it. Is there any way we can get her out of here?"

"Well, no. Not unless a relative or legal guardian picks her up."

"Then I'll sneak her out. Where is she?"

"You're not going to sneak her out, Gannon," my mom said sternly.

"Well, can she leave for the day or something? Even for a few hours? Under adult supervision, of course. We need you to come with us too."

"Gannon, this is all so sudden."

"I need you to trust me, Mom. A lot of people are counting on us. Please. Ask if we can take Grace over to Parliament for the morning. Just say it's a field trip. You wouldn't be lying. Come on, they have to allow it."

"Actually they do, Gannon. In fact, they encourage it as long as there is an adult to chaperone."

"Then please help us, Mom."

"If it means this much to you, I'll see what I can do."

Okay, let me just say that my mom rocks! And I'm not

just saying that because I know she's going to read my journal either. I really mean it! Fifteen minutes hadn't passed before she came walking back into the lobby with Grace at her side. As soon as Grace saw me, she ran across the room and gave me the biggest hug, which was totally awesome, of course.

"It's so good to see you, Gannon!" she said.

"Good to see you too. Listen, Wyatt and I have a plan to save your farm and to help your dad, too. We just need to get to Leinster House. We're meeting Wyatt outside the gates."

"We can take the tram," she said.

"Okay, let's go," I said. "I'll fill you in on the way."

So, could be that I'm a bit loopy from sleeping on a cold bench, but I have a feeling that I've finally been blessed with the "Luck of the Irish." I mean, I've kissed the Blarney Stone, had a fairy tell me that all of Ireland is counting on us, discovered a four-leaf clover, and laid my hands upon statues of two of Ireland's most famous writers. Besides that, I'm 25 percent Irish! Really, what else could I possibly do? I think I've earned some of that good ol' Irish luck. And if there was ever a day I needed it, it's today!

WYATT

OCTOBER 10, 5:28 PM
DUBLIN, IRELAND   53° 20′ N   6° 15′ W
53° FAHRENHEIT, 12° CELSIUS

Leinster House, Irish Parliament, Dublin

The Irish National Parliament is housed on an impressive campus that spans several blocks. The buildings exude the power that I suppose a house of government should, with gray stone walls, arched entryways, grand pillars, and a towering octagonal dome with a clock underneath. Elaborate statues stand like guardians on the corners of rooftops.

Crossing Kildare Street I saw Gannon, my mom, and Grace waiting outside the wrought iron gates near a guard station. I had all the photographs in my backpack and was ready to drop off a set in each member's office. I just wasn't so sure how we were going to get inside. There were guards everywhere and they weren't letting people through the gates.

"It's so good to see you, Wyatt!" my mom said, squeezing me in a tight hug.

"Good to see you too, Mom."

"Gannon tells me you have some important photographs that you want to deliver to the members of Parliament."

"That's right," I said.

"Well, as long as it's done tactfully," my mom said, "I don't see a problem with it."

"I'm curious why they have this place closed off this morning," Gannon said. "Hey, Mom. Would you mind asking the guard what time the grounds open up to the public?"

"I'd be happy to."

"Oh, and while you have his ear, get as much info as you can on the place. You know, brochures with the history and whatnot. I want to add lots of good info to my journal."

"Great idea, Gannon. I'll do that."

When my mom walked off, Gannon quickly turned to us.

"As soon as Mom engages the guard in conversation, we're going in."

"What? No way." I said.

"If we get caught, we'll say we didn't know any better. We're kids. The gate was open. We just walked in. No harm done, right?"

"Sorry, I'm not doing it."

"Grace, are you coming with me?" Gannon asked.

"Of course I am," she said without hesitation.

"Look, the guard's totally distracted," Gannon said, pointing. "It's go time!"

Gannon and Grace casually slipped in the gate and ran down a hallway that led into the courtyard. I was reluctant at first but felt obligated to keep my brother from doing something stupid, so I ran to catch up.

Across the courtyard, we walked through two massive doors and into Leinster House. Across the room was a woman seated at a desk.

"Wait here," Gannon said and approached her.

"This is where we get kicked out," I said to Grace.

A minute later Gannon came back with a huge smile on his face.

"You're not going to believe this," he said. "Parliament is in session!"

"You're kidding?" Grace said.

"The woman said it's actually an emergency joint session," he added.

"What does that mean exactly?" I asked.

"Basically, it means that everyone who's anyone in Ireland's government is here right now!" Gannon said, jumping up and down with excitement. "Come on, I want to get inside before they start!"

"Wait, are you saying you want to go inside the chambers?"

"I already got the okay. Told the woman we're students from America on a field trip and that we'd love to get a glimpse of how the Irish government works."

"And she bought that?"

"Not only did she buy it, she told me there's an observation deck where we can sit and watch the session."

"I don't think this is such a good idea. I say we just leave the photos in each member's office and follow up tomorrow."

"No way, Wyatt. Every member of the House of Commons and the House of Lords is filing into the chambers right now! We couldn't have asked for a better opportunity to present our case!"

"That's the thing. We're not prepared to present our case. I already told you, Gannon. We need to construct our argument and formulate a well-thought-out statement. It needs to be written and rehearsed . . ."

"Sorry, Wyatt. I'm done talking about this," Gannon said. "I'll meet you inside."

At that, he took off running for the chambers.

"I can't believe this is happening," I said to Grace. "I'm afraid we're going to witness a repeat of his outburst at Dromoland Castle."

"He's just trying to do what's right," Grace said. "You can't fault him for that. Let's catch up. Maybe he has a plan."

"Trust me, he never has a plan."

Inside the expansive chambers was a horseshoe-shaped auditorium lined with dark wooden desks and oversized chairs for each member. High above, built into the ceiling, was a white dome that seemed to be illuminated by the sunlight. I was swept up in the grandeur of the chambers, when all of a sudden, horror struck. Looking across the room, I saw my brother. He was approaching the podium!

"Oh, no," I said, terrified. "What's he doing?"

"Looks like he plans to have a word with the members," Grace said.

"But why are they just letting him walk right up there? Seriously, someone has to stop him."

Maybe a young kid walking into Parliament seemed so harmless the members simply chose to ignore him. I honestly don't know, but whatever the case, nobody prevented Gannon from taking his place at the podium—the same podium used by the Irish prime minister and leaders from around the world. I had actually seen a photograph of U.S. President John F. Kennedy speaking from the very spot where my brother now stood.

Gannon adjusted the microphone, cleared his throat.

"Ladies and gentlemen," he said, his voice echoing through the chambers, "honorable members of the Irish Parliament."

"This can't be happening," I said.

"Before you begin your very important work today, whatever that may be, I humbly ask for a minute of your time."

Members of Parliament looked around at one another, obviously wondering what this kid was doing up there. Others continued with their own business, completely ignoring the stranger speaking to them. When it became clear that Gannon might actually be allowed to continue, I realized it was up to me to stop him. But before I could take two steps, Grace grabbed me by the arm.

"You have to give him a chance," she said.

"You don't know my brother like I do. Trust me, he's going to make a fool of himself and ruin everything."

"Please, Wyatt. I can tell how deeply he cares about our farm, about the animals and the land. You both do. You wouldn't have gone to all of this trouble if it weren't important to you. Let your brother speak from the heart. It may actually do some good."

As much as I wanted to yank Gannon away from the microphone, I wasn't going to argue with Grace. It was her family's livelihood that was being threatened. It was her farm and the farms of her neighbors that were at risk. If she wanted to give Gannon a chance to help, who was I to say no? No matter how certain I was that his speech was going to be a complete disaster, Grace was right; it wasn't my place to stop it.

Gannon continued, "As you might have gathered from my accent, I am not Irish. However, I am the great-grandson of a couple from Castlewellan. A hard-working couple. Farmers who, I've come to learn, had a deep love of the Irish countryside and its people. Though I may not be full-blooded Irish by birth, my great-grandparents' love of this country has been passed down through the generations. I felt it sweep over me the second I stepped off the plane. I felt it as we traveled through the beautiful countryside and visited my ancestors' hometown. I felt it as my brother and I worked the land, tending crops at Shamrock Farm in County Kerry. And it is because of this deep connection I have with Ireland, this love of your country, that I must speak out against a terrible injustice. Ladies and gentlemen of Parliament, Ireland is being poisoned."

Gannon paused and looked around the chambers like a true head of state. Most members of Parliament had stopped scurrying about and were now paying close attention. They actually *wanted* to hear what my brother had to say.

"Now, I know you are all well aware that there are many businesses in this country and around the world that are polluting the environment," he continued. "Most governments have measures in place that tell us how much each is polluting. And those within 'safe levels' are allowed to continue operating. Of course, in this case, the term 'safe' can be debated. There is really no such thing as 'safe' pollution. All pollution is harmful. But I am not here to debate that. I am here to make you aware of a man who seems to be operating above the law. A man who is deliberately and illegally contaminating Ireland's air and water. A man who is treating tens of thousands of animals cruelly and unethically. A man who is committing horrible crimes against nature. A man who, if left unchecked, will singlehandedly create an environmental disaster the likes of which this country has never seen. The man I speak of is Mr. Kilgore Moloney, owner of Moloney Factory Farm Complex."

Obviously the name was well known, as there was a low rumble of discussion in the chambers.

"Whether he's paying county officials to help keep his dirty secret from Ireland's Environmental Protection Agency or not is up to you to determine. The thing that must be addressed immediately is the catastrophic damage being done right this very minute as a result of his operations. My brother, Wyatt, who is standing in the back, has the proof in his backpack. Water samples showing toxin levels that are off the charts. Air quality tests proving that Mr. Moloney is contaminating the air Irish citizens breathe. Photographs and video showing the atrocious conditions in which the animals are imprisoned. Wyatt, please distribute the photographs so everyone here can take a good look."

I asked Grace to help and we did as Gannon requested, handing out stacks of photos and asking that the members pass them around. Judging by the shock on their faces, the members of Parliament were appalled at what they saw.

"You can verify our test results in the labs of the Irish EPA, but I can assure you, the results will be the same. My brother is an expert at this stuff, and I'm proud to say that when it comes to scientific testing, he does not make mistakes."

I have to admit, Gannon's compliment in front of such a distinguished crowd was unexpected and appreciated.

"I don't know very many quotes by heart, but this one by George Bernard Shaw has stuck with me: 'If there was nothing wrong in the world there would be nothing for us to do.'"

The chamber broke out in laughter. Gannon chuckled too.

"I mean, none of us would be here right now if that weren't true, am I right? But in all seriousness, there are things that are wrong in the world. Unfortunately, many, many things. The Moloney Factory Farm Complex happens to be one of those things, and we have to do something about it!"

Parliament erupted in applause.

"'Tis as if he kissed the Blarney Stone," Grace said, gazing with admiration at my brother. "He truly has the gift of gab."

I shook my head in utter disbelief.

"'Tis as if he had," I said.

As the applause went on, I felt someone grab ahold of my arm.

"I knew I'd find ya!" came a voice in my ear.

It was the security guard we had slipped past. He was also clutching Grace. My mom was standing next to the man, looking terribly disappointed.

"How could you go sneaking off like that?" she asked. "You knew we weren't allowed through those gates."

My mom's reprimand would have continued if her attention hadn't been diverted to the podium.

"Oh my gosh," she said. "Please tell me that's not Gannon up there?"

"Okay, I won't. But it is."

When the guard saw Gannon, he released his grip on us and charged forward with every intention of removing him from the podium. But before he got very far, Grace ran around and cut him off.

"As you can plainly see, members of Parliament have permitted him to speak," Grace said sternly. "And it seems they are appreciating what he has to say. I would advise you not to cause a scene, lest your mistake of letting three kids sneak into the chambers be brought to light in front of everyone."

This gave the security guard immediate pause.

"A fine point, young lady," he said. "I suppose I shall allow him to continue. But the moment he concludes, you will be escorted from the chamber. The public is not allowed on the floor. Only in the observation balcony."

"That will be fine."

When the applause quieted, Gannon delivered a passionate plea.

"Ladies and gentlemen," he said, "in County Kerry, Irish eyes are crying because their green grasses are dying. Local farmers are suffering. Nature is suffering. And to remedy this, swift action must be taken. So, in closing, I have but one favor to ask. I ask that you send a member of Ireland's EPA to inspect Mr. Moloney's operation, and I request that it be done today, before he gets word that they are coming. I am fully confident that a surprise inspection will confirm everything I have told you and provide more than enough evidence to have his entire operation shut down, effective immediately. Thank you all so much for giving me the chance to speak before you here today. It has been a real honor."

The chamber erupted in cheers. Gannon nodded and smiled proudly, enjoying every moment. Just before he stepped away from the podium, he threw his fist into the air and shouted:

"Éirinn go Brách!"

Everyone in the chamber threw their arms into the air and repeated the phrase, Grace and the security guard included. Loud applause continued as Gannon walked down the aisle, waving to members like some distinguished world leader. When he finally reached us in the back, he leaned in close to my ear.

"Éirinn go Brách means Ireland Forever," he whispered.

"Póg amach, Gannon," I replied.

Gannon laughed.

"So you finally learned what that means, huh?" he said.

"I asked the guy at the photo shop. Told him that you kept saying it to me. He said, 'Mate, I hate to tell you this, but póg amach means *kiss off.*'"

Gannon and I both laughed.

"Gannon," my mom said, grabbing him by the shoulders, "I don't know what to do with you."

"Sorry we had to ditch you like that, Mom," he said, "but as you can see we had some pretty important stuff to do."

"Well that doesn't excuse the fact that you made a poor

decision. You could have gotten yourself in big trouble. At the same time, I'm so proud of what you are all trying to do. It's very admirable."

"Well, before we go around patting ourselves on the back," Gannon said, "we have one more thing left to do."

"What's that?" my mom asked.

"Reunite Grace with her father!"

Apparently, Gannon's gift of gab is the kind of gift that keeps on giving, because he somehow wound up convincing the orphanage to release Grace for twenty-four hours, provided my mother act as her chaperone and take full responsibility for returning her the next day. We're hoping that she won't have to go back at all, but that depends on whether or not we can get Mr. O'Leary out of prison. We're all back on the bus, rolling through the green pastures of southern Ireland on our way to the County Kerry courthouse to see what we can do.

GANNON
OCTOBER 11

If I told Wyatt once, I told him a thousand times. Whatever you believe, you can achieve. I mean, no matter how bad it got, I never gave up faith that the "gift of gab" would finally kick in and help make things right for the O'Learys, the farmers in County Kerry, and the people of Ireland. And, sure enough, that's exactly what happened!

Within hours of my eloquent and heartfelt speech, the Irish EPA sent a group of scientists to conduct an unannounced inspection of the Moloney Factory Farm Complex. According to *The Irish Times*, Kilgore Moloney had such a fit that he got himself arrested on the spot. Better yet, the complex has been shut down until they can determine just how much environmental damage he's caused, at which time he will be forced to pay for the cleanup. Oh, and here's some more awesome news, all of Moloney's livestock is going to be auctioned off to local farmers, so the animals will be free to graze the lush Irish grasslands, the way nature intended.

As for Mr. O'Leary, well, it took some serious slick talking and a tearful plea from Grace, not to mention some bail money, but we were finally able to convince the Garda to release him from that dingy jail cell. And, wow, what a reunion it was! Just like the kind you see in the movies. When Mr. O came through the door and saw Grace, we all just about burst into tears.

"Come here, sweetheart," Mr. O'Leary said.

Grace ran for her dad and jumped into his arms.

"Oh, Grace," Mr. O'Leary said. "I thought I had lost you. I am so sorry. I hope you'll forgive me."

"On one condition," she said, tears streaming down her cheeks.

"Name it."

"Just promise me you'll never do anything so incredibly foolish again."

"Oh, I promise, Gracie. Never again."

Grace gathered herself, drying tears with her sleeve.

"Da, can we go home?"

"Yes, sweetheart. We can go home."

"I love you, Da."

"I love you too, Gracie."

Now, it's not like Mr. O'Leary is getting off without punishment. He'll still have to go to court and face the music, so to speak. What'll keep him from going back to jail, we were told, is the fact that his actions were pretty well justified. I mean, he was freeing animals that were being terribly mistreated and forced to live in horrific conditions, so the argument can be made that Mr. O'Leary was simply taking justice into his own hands.

"It has been an experience, lads," Mr. O'Leary said of the past couple days. "An experience I certainly learned from."

"You know what Oscar Wilde said, Da?" Grace added. "Experience is the name everyone gives to their mistakes."

"Clever chap, that Oscar Wilde," Mr. O'Leary said, laughing. "Clever indeed."

Back at the O'Leary's farmhouse, my mom handed out steaming mugs of Irish tea. Mr. O'Leary lifted his mug.

"Sláinte," he said.

"Sláinte," my mom repeated.

"Sláinte means—"

"Good health," Wyatt said, cutting me off.

"Ah, you're finally picking up some of the Gaelic language. I'm impressed, bro."

The next morning my dad arrived from the Dingle Peninsula, his backseat filled to the roof with painted canvases. I stepped off the porch to greet him as he climbed out of the car. He was waving a newspaper around in the air.

"Your mom explained everything to me, but that didn't prepare me for this," he said, handing me the paper.

Lo and behold, who was on the front page, but yours truly!

"Wow, what a good-looking chap," I said, pointing at my picture.

Wyatt walked over and read the headline.

"Unlikely Hero Wins Victory for the Environment."

"Unlikely hero?" I asked. "What's so 'unlikely' about me being a hero?"

"I think it was a fair choice of words," Wyatt said.

"I hope you boys realize that this could have turned out really bad for you," my dad said. "If you had been caught on Moloney's farm or caught sneaking into Parliament, you might have found yourselves facing some serious charges."

"It was worth the risk, Dad," I said. "If you want to accomplish big things, you have to take big risks, right?"

"I'm pretty sure I've said that before," Wyatt chimed in. "I think you're recycling my material."

"Don't even try to take credit for my eloquence. You want the gift of gab, you're going to have to go back and kiss the Blarney Stone yourself."

Wyatt just rolled his eyes.

"You know, this newspaper article is great and all," I said, "but it only tells part of the story."

"Well, I want to know the whole story," my dad said. "So, which one of you is going to tell it to me?"

"Follow us inside, Dad. We'll give you our journals. Wyatt and I worked really hard to get it all down on paper. And it's a pretty thrilling tale, if I do say so myself."

"I bet it is," my dad said. "I bet it is."

WYATT

OCTOBER 13, 5:28 PM
SHAMROCK FARM, COUNTY KERRY
56° FAHRENHEIT, 13° CELSIUS
SUNNY, WIND CALM

An Irish party is something you have to experience to fully understand. There's lots of eating and toasts and pints of Guinness clanking, conversation and laugher, music and dancing. The decibel level continues to ramp up the later the party goes on, and this one went late.

Hundreds showed up from all across the county to celebrate the closing of Moloney's Factory Farm Complex and to thank Mr. O'Leary for his courageous act.

"It isn't me who deserves all the thanks," Mr. O'Leary said, speaking to the crowd from his porch. "I would like to introduce everyone to a couple of brave young men. Gannon and Wyatt, please step up here for a moment." We walked up the steps of the porch, blushing slightly as we looked out at all the smiling faces. "I initially thought these boys were far too delicate to last a single day on this farm," Mr. O'Leary continued, getting a good laugh out of everyone. "But they proved me wrong. We all owe them a debt of gratitude for their willingness to take a stand. They helped stop the polluting, helped protect our environment, our forests, rivers, air, and wildlife. When you boil it down, what they really did was protect our way of life! A way of life we all love and cherish!"

Everyone clapped, whistled, and hollered.

"Would you like to say anything, boys?" Mr. O'Leary asked.

"You won't believe this, but I'm kind of at a loss for words," Gannon said. "Must have used up my gift of gab. Wyatt, why don't you say something for us?"

I turned to the crowd and said the first thing that came to mind.

"If you're lucky enough to be Irish . . . You're lucky enough!"

"Well said, lad!" someone shouted.

"Sláinte," another said.

Everyone else raised their glasses.

A traditional Irish band set up near the barn and began to play, while people from all over the county danced in the pasture. There were three violinists, a banjo, a mandolin, an accordion, and a bodhrán, which is a handheld drum. The energy of good Irish music is contagious. The upbeat tempo lifts the spirits, makes you want to move. It's feel-good music.

I must admit, I'm not a very good dancer, but I couldn't help myself and did my best to cut an Irish jig.

Everyone who showed up brought a dish of food. There was so much it filled a table that had to be fifty feet long. We had potatoes made every which way, beef, bacon, and cabbage, bowls of thick gravy and pots of Irish stew, blood sausage, fried trout and fresh salmon, pans of shepherd's pie, all kinds of cheeses, soda bread, and delicious Banoffee pies for dessert.

A sweet Banoffee pie

As the sun dropped on the horizon and the sky turned a reddish-gold, I weaved my way through the crowd and took a seat on the steps of the porch. Looking out over the farm,

I was struck by a great feeling of accomplishment. We certainly made some mistakes along the way, but as Mr. O'Leary said, Gannon and I had played a critical role in the future of this beautiful place. It wasn't easy, but things worth fighting for are never easy. What's most important is that you find the courage to stand up for what's right. If you do, you'll feel good knowing you did your part to make the world a better place. It was my brother, Gannon, who taught me that.

GANNON

SHAMROCK FARM

Historic Provisional Document of the Irish Republic

Over the course of this country's storied history, the Irish have endured serious hardships—invasions, wars, plagues, famines—but despite these terrible misfortunes the Irish have survived, forged ahead, even thrived.

A tough, resilient lot, the Irish are also full of compassion, humor, and good cheer. Lots of writers describe the Irish as people who live with a constant sense of tragedy and sorrow, but during our time here I haven't found that to be true at all. The Irish people I've met have been funny, intelligent, and bursting with pride for their country. And after last night's party, I can also say this for the Irish: They sure do know how to have a good time! In my opinion, the Irish people themselves are one of the country's greatest treasures.

This morning I woke early and put on my rain boots and took a stroll down to the O'Leary's pond. Still a little groggy after such a late night, it felt good to fill my head with the morning's crisp air. The smell of peat logs came from the farmhouse chimney. A blanket of steam swirled atop the surface of the pond, where several swans had returned to swim. The sky was equal parts gray and blue, with beams of sun burning through gaps in the cloud cover, bringing light to Ireland's forty different shades of green. On the far end of the farm the river ran, already cleaner and sparkling in places where the water's ripples met the sun's first rays.

It was nice to be alone in the quiet morning, just me and my thoughts. But who am I kidding, I like company and was thrilled when Oscar paid a visit, swooping over the farm and coming to rest in the high branches of the Scots pine.

As I stared up at this beautiful tree, tall and full and healthy, with Oscar proudly surveying his territory, I thought of the photo Grace had shown us of Mrs. O'Leary planting it as a child. The tree was so small at the time, hardly more than a twig. So thin and fragile, in fact, I wouldn't have guessed it would survive its first winter. And now, to see it all these years later, standing so strong and stoic, it made me think.

Like the Irish people, nature is resilient.

Nature finds a way.

Nature will endure.

But nature needs a helping hand.

To end this journal entry on a positive note, I'll say that I have a whole lot of faith in our generation. Not to brag or anything, but let's face it, we're pretty awesome. And I think we're growing up with a good understanding of the problems we face. I think we're good-hearted and curious and smart and will come up with creative solutions that will put us on the right track. With a little cooperation on our part, we can live in harmony with nature. We can make things better. Better for the earth. Better for us. Better for generations to come.

As originally promised, we're staying on for another couple weeks to finish our work at Shamrock Farm. My parents are pitching in, too. They'll be planting several hundred new trees to assist the reforestation project and helping prep the soil for winter. Today, Mr. O'Leary said we're going to shear a few sheep, which I think will be a pretty cool experience.

It's all important work, and even though I'm sure I'll complain about some of it from time to time, truth is, I'm actually honored to do it. And, hey, I'll be honest, getting to spend more time with Grace is a huge bonus. She's even going to take us to the School of Falconry at Ashford Castle were we can learn to become expert falconers. I mean, how awesome is that going to be?

So, until we begin our next adventure, I think I'll put away my journal and give this beautiful countryside my full, complete, and undivided attention.

Éirinn go Brách!

Swans taking a morning swim

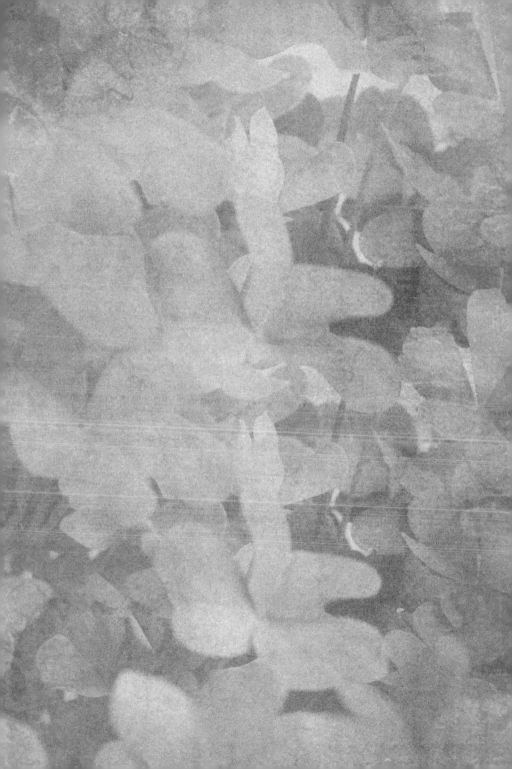

AUTHORS' NOTE

It's probably pretty clear to those who read this book just how much we enjoyed visiting Ireland. The scenery in parts of the country—the Dingle Peninsula being one of our favorites— is absolutely breathtaking. The Irish people are warmhearted, proud, and love to have a good time. Many of our literary heroes hailed from the Emerald Isle. It is also the country of our ancestry. Growing up, our grandparents told us many stories of Ireland. We imagined it as a sort of dreamscape, a place were you might actually have a brush with magic.

Given all there is to this relatively small nation—and there is so much—one thing stayed with us long after we left: a piece of Ireland's history that's still hard to compre- hend. As we crisscrossed the country, we came across several monuments dedicated to the Great Famine, which took the lives of over one million people. To hear stories of orphaned children knocking on doors, only to be denied entrance because it just wasn't possible to feed another person, left us heartbroken. Witnessing Ireland's prosperity today, the busy restaurants, pubs, shops, the productive farms, and beautiful countryside, it seems almost unfathomable that such a thing could have happened. And yet, it did.

Bearing witness to the history of the Great Famine is another example of the profound lessons one receives through travel—a lesson that puts life in perspective and teaches us to never take for granted the things we have. Seeing the monuments of the emaciated men, women, and children was a reminder that those of us who have quick and easy access to food are truly fortunate.

Of course, not all parts of the world enjoy this luxury. Millions still suffer from hunger today, and the world's population continues to grow. Herein lies the challenge. How do we feed more and more people and do so in an ethical manner? In our haste to provide, some have chosen to neglect and even mistreat the animals that ultimately feed us, to pollute, and produce food that is unhealthy to those who consume it. Farmers must deal with issues of volume and efficiency. Not to mention make a profit. All legitimate concerns. So, what's the solution? We don't know. What we do know is that there are humane and healthy ways to go about it.

Our goal with each Travels with Gannon & Wyatt book is to entertain and educate young readers and to leave them with a vivid and authentic picture of a special place. Maybe we'll even inspire them to take a trip there one day. Beyond that, the books subtly introduce young readers to a variety of global issues. We do this for a reason. Bringing these stories to the imaginations of readers may help lead a small number of children to his or her passion, his or her purpose in life. We know it sounds lofty, but that is our aim, for those who discover their passion have the power to change the world.

ACKNOWLEDGMENTS

Given both of our families have Irish lineage, this is a very special book for us. So, who better to honor first than our Irish ancestors. They include John A. Wheeler, Thomas and Margaret McAlea of Castlewellan, and Keith's beautiful and witty grandmother, Mary Hemstreet. Tracing our family history in Ireland was an experience that touched us deeply. Words cannot express the gratitude we have for Frankie Gause, Patti's mother, who turned one hundred years old this year. An avid traveler herself, Frankie has kept a journal for over eighty years. Your influence is at the core of each and every book we write. Thank you to our eloquent guide, Martin, who kept us informed and entertained from Belfast to Killarney, and to Jake Gallaher and Luke Seamans who kept us laughing from Galway to Dublin. Finally, a special thank you to one of the world's great environmental advocates, Robert F. Kennedy Jr. As the Chairman of the Waterkeeper Alliance and one of *Time* magazine's "Heroes for the Planet," we often turn to your work for inspiration. It is truly an honor to have your endorsement.

GANNON & WYATT's

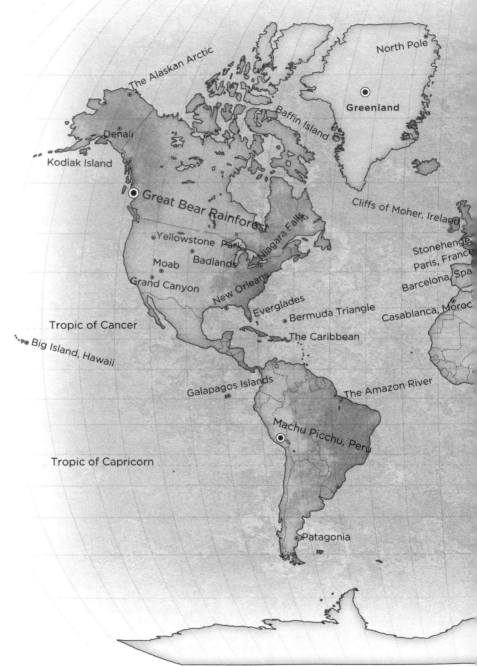

The Alaskan Arctic

North Pole

Greenland

Baffin Island

Denali

Kodiak Island

Cliffs of Moher, Ireland

Great Bear Rainforest

Yellowstone Park

Niagara Falls

Stonehenge
Paris, France

Moab   Badlands

Barcelona, Spa

Grand Canyon

New Orleans

Casablanca, Moroc

Everglades

Tropic of Cancer

Bermuda Triangle

The Caribbean

Big Island, Hawaii

Galapagos Islands

The Amazon River

Machu Picchu, Peru

Tropic of Capricorn

Patagonia

TRAVEL MAP

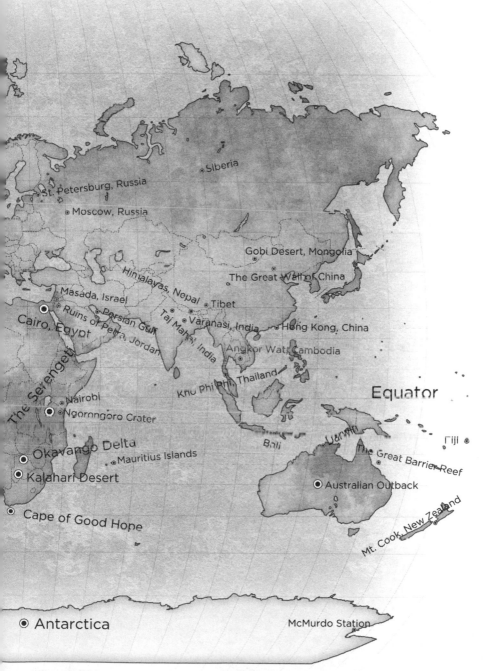

Siberia

St. Petersburg, Russia

Moscow, Russia

Gobi Desert, Mongolia

The Great Wall of China

Himalayas, Nepal

Masada, Israel

Tibet

Ruins of Petra, Jordan

Persian Gulf

Taj Mahal, India

Varanasi, India

Hong Kong, China

Cairo, Egypt

Angkor Wat, Cambodia

The Serengeti

Kho Phi Phi, Thailand

Equator

Nairobi

Ngorongoro Crater

Okavango Delta

Bali

Uluru

Fiji

Mauritius Islands

The Great Barrier Reef

Kalahari Desert

Australian Outback

Cape of Good Hope

Mt. Cook, New Zealand

Antarctica

McMurdo Station

Gannon and Wyatt in Ireland

MEET THE "REAL-LIFE" GANNON AND WYATT

Have you ever imagined traveling the world over? Fifteen-year-old twin brothers Gannon and Wyatt have done just that. With a flight attendant for a mom and an international businessman for a dad, the spirit of adventure has been nurtured in them since they were very young. When they got older, the globetrotting brothers had an idea—why not share all of the amazing things they've learned during their travels with other kids? The result is the book series, Travels with Gannon & Wyatt, a video web series, blog, photographs from all over the world, and much more. Furthering their mission, the brothers also cofounded the Youth Exploration Society (Y.E.S.), an organization of young people who are passionate about making the world a better place. Each Travels with Gannon & Wyatt book is loosely based on real-life travels. Gannon and Wyatt have actually been to Greenland and run dog sleds on the ice sheet. They have kissed the Blarney Stone in Ireland, investigated Mayan temples in Mexico, and explored the active volcanoes of Hawaii. During these "research missions," the authors, along with Gannon and Wyatt, often sit around the campfire collaborating on an adventure tale that sets two young explorers on a quest for the kind of knowledge you can't get from a textbook. We hope you enjoy the novels that were inspired by these fireside chats. As Gannon and Wyatt like to say, "The world is our classroom, and we're bringing you along."

HAPPY TRAVELS!

Want to become a member of the
Youth Exploration Society
just like Gannon and Wyatt?

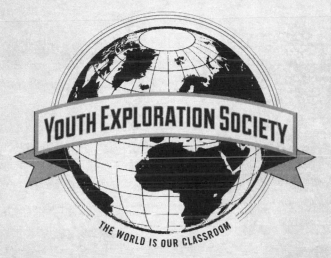

Check out our website. That's where you'll learn how to become a member of the Youth Exploration Society, an organization of young people, like yourself, who love to travel and are interested in world geography, cultures, and wildlife.

The website also includes:

Cool facts about every country on earth, a gallery of the world's flags, a world map where you can learn about different cultures and wildlife, spectacular photos from all corners of the globe, and information about Y.E.S. programs.

BE SURE TO CHECK IT OUT!
WWW.YOUTHEXPLORATIONSOCIETY.ORG

ABOUT THE AUTHORS

PATTI WHEELER, producer of the web series *Travels with Gannon & Wyatt: Off the Beaten Path*, began traveling at a young age and has nurtured the spirit of adventure in her family ever since. For years it has been her goal to create children's books that instill the spirit of adventure in young people. The Youth Exploration Society and *Travels with Gannon & Wyatt* are the realization of her dream.

KEITH HEMSTREET is a writer, producer, and cofounder of the Youth Exploration Society. He attended Florida State University and completed his graduate studies at Appalachian State University. He lives in Aspen, Colorado, with his wife and three daughters.

Make sure to check out the first four books in our
award-winning series:

Botswana

Great Bear Rainforest

Egypt

Greenland

Look for upcoming books and video from these and
other exciting locations:

Hawaii

Mexico

Australia

Iceland

The American West

Don't forget to check out our website:

WWW.GANNONANDWYATT.COM

There you'll find complete episodes of our award-winning
web series shot on location with Gannon & Wyatt.

You'll also find a gallery with spectacular photographs
from Greenland, Iceland, Egypt, the Great Bear Rainforest,
and Botswana.

And wait, one more thing . . .

Check us out on Twitter, Pinterest, and
make sure to "like" us on Facebook!
With your parents' permission, of course.

Praise for *Travels with Gannon & Wyatt*

Each of us has the responsibility to protect and enrich our community, to ensure that future generations inherit a healthy and vibrant planet. In each action-packed book, *Travels with Gannon & Wyatt* communicates these values and inspires young people to do their part to help make the world a better place.

—Robert F. Kennedy Jr. (Travels with Gannon & Wyatt Series)

Wheeler and Hemstreet pack this slim adventure full of facts and trivia, as well as photos and drawings, lending it an educational slant. With clear nods to Indiana Jones and other adventure stories, the fast-paced plot and engaging characters are sure to appeal to a young audience.   **—Publishers Weekly** (Egypt)

Twin teens explore various locations and introduce readers to the wonders, animals, and people of the places they visit. The books have a strong conservationist point of view, and the siblings encounter trouble not only from their natural surroundings but also from man-made threats to themselves and the environment. Each book also contains native people who help Gannon and Wyatt understand the areas they are exploring and, in some cases, help them survive… the books focus primarily on painting a picture of the boys' travels and surroundings, and they do this well. The novels offer good entry points into these exciting worlds and should be enjoyed by anyone who likes reading about adventure and discovery.

—School Library Journal (Botswana, Great Bear Rainforest)

This is the brilliant first of what I hope will be many in a travel-novel series . . . Botswana has rarely had a portrayal that so accurately captures the physical and spiritual spirit of Africa.

—Sacramento Book Review (Botswana)

Young, would-be adventurers or armchair travelers will enjoy exploring with these two straightforward, engaging personalities—and will learn a lot in the process.

—**Kirkus Discoveries** (Botswana)

Written in the grand tradition of the Hardy Boys, Tom Swift, and Willard Price's adventure-seeking brothers Hal and Roger Hunt.

—**Michelle Mallette**, Librarian and Blogger, Michelle's Bookshelf (Great Bear Rainforest)

It's the best book I've ever read! —**Anna**, 10 (Botswana)

Travels with Gannon & Wyatt is a groundbreaking series of adventurous stories like nothing else ever seen in children's literature.

—**Mark Zeiler**, Middle School Language Arts Teacher, Orlando, Florida (Travels with Gannon & Wyatt Series)

I loved the first three books! Egypt was my favorite and I can't wait to read Greenland.

—**Kipp**, 9 (Egypt)

A top-notch tale of adventure! Reading *Travels with Gannon & Wyatt Botswana* was like taking a journey into the heart of Africa.

—**John Kingsley-Heath**, Former Asst. Director of Uganda's National Parks

Travels with Gannon & Wyatt Botswana is phenomenal! I read it in three hours!

—**Felix**, 9 (Botswana)

MY JOURNAL NOTES